From The Sea Come Seashells

By Larry Hobson

Table of Contents

Dedication

This book is dedicated to

Victoria Elizabeth Hobson,

my lovely wife who died

November 7, 2022

Chapter 1

Normally, life begins at conception. Though created equal, once born, all children are not given an equal opportunity in life. Some do not go home to a loving mother and father as they deserve to. This is the unfortunate case for Steven Mars.

Steven's mother died while birthing him, and he never knew his father because his dad abandoned his mother early in her pregnancy. Steven grew up never seeing a mother's smiling face or experiencing a mother's unconditional love. He never had the father that all young boys need in their life.

Steven was born in a small town in Ohio on May 5, 1951. Having lived with several different foster parents, as his maternal grandfather was located in the desert town of Mojave, California. After interviews and several visits from county social services and child welfare departments, the government concluded that Henry was able to provide his grandson with a safe and loving environment.

In June 1957, Steven, now 6-years-old, was put on a train to Barstow, California, to live with a person he did not know. Told he was going to live with family, Steven had no idea what the word "family" meant; he only understood being moved from one foster home to another. The social worker in Ohio taking Steven to the train station explained that going to California to live with his grandfather was his chance to have a permanent home to call his own. This made Steven feel hopeful for a better life.

Steven's grandfather's name was Henry Benson. Henry was born in 1900 and raised in Cambria, a town located along California's central coast. Cambria is where Steven's mother, Ashley, was born and raised as well, until running away in 1948 when she was 17 years old, never to return.

Henry moved to Mojave in 1954, the year he retired, and the year he lost his wife of 30 years, Victoria, to cancer. Cambria had good and bad memories for Henry, but at this time in his life all memories seemed bad. Living all alone in the home where his wife died was too emotionally painful.

He chose Mojave because the region was known for its gold deposits. Henry decided to spend his retirement wandering around the hillsides under the always blue skies of Southern California's High Desert, forgetting about the past and keeping himself busy by mining for the gilded precious metal. Now with his 6-year-old grandson coming to live with him, Henry's mining days were over.

As the train pulled into Mojave station, Steven saw an old man in his mid- '50s standing alone on the platform. When the train came to a stop, Henry saw a little boy's scared face looking at him from inside the passenger car. The steward took hold of Steven's hand and suitcase and led him down the three steps to the pavement below. The scared look of a child and a smile on the face of an old man said it all. For Henry, looking at Steven was like seeing his daughter again.

"Hello, steward. I'm Henry Benson," said Henry.

"Hello, Mr. Benson. This is Steven," said the steward, as he let go of Steven's hand and gently guided the boy toward his grandfather's side. "Good luck to you, sir. Good luck to you both."

Henry took Steven by his hand, picked up the boy's suitcase, and walked his grandson to his car, a blue 1949 Plymouth, for the ride home. Steven sat as close as he could to the passenger door, eyes focused on scenery completely new to him. He had lived in the country where the landscape is green, except when it is white and covered with snow. Ohio has many trees and the land is dotted by farmhouses. Now all Steven saw was myriad shades of brown, blowing sand, scrub, and Joshua trees.

Driving west on Highway 58, Steven noticed barren hills and small houses. He was curious about the homes but too shy to ask about them. Had he asked, his grandfather would have told him that miners lived in the homes, and if he looked closely he would see dark spots along the hillside, which were the entrances to mining shafts.

Bored with the landscape and curious about this man his social worker in Ohio referred to as "grandfather," the eyes of the small child now moved from the right to the left where his grandfather sat behind the steering wheel, eyes glued on the road ahead. Just as the lens of a movie camera records all that is placed in front of it, Steven was recording the actions of this strange old man sitting next to him. What is a grandfather to a child that doesn't even know what a mother or father is? All

Steven understood is that he is being moved, once again, to another strange place.

Both Steven and Henry were silent during the one-hour car ride home. When Henry pulled into the driveway and parked, he said, "This is it. This is our house. This is your new home, Steven."

Steven did not know what to say when he saw the old, brown bungalow with no grass lawn to roll around on. The only tree was a solitary Chinese Elm planted to the west to put the house in late-afternoon shade during intense summer heat. It looked unlike any house he had lived in.

To Steven, it did not seem as if things were getting better. Many thoughts raced through Steven's mind; thoughts he kept to himself: Was it something I did or say that brought me here? I must be a bad child to be moved around so often. Nobody wants me. How long until I move again? Where will I go next? These were the thoughts occupying Steven's mind.

When the car stopped and Henry turned off the motor and got out of the car, Steven did not open his car door but instead sat inside, staring at the house. Henry walked around the car and opened Steven's door, signaling for Steven to climb out.

"It's hot," Steven said, head and eyes down.

"Yes, it is," answered Henry. "Not to worry. It's cold inside the house. I, I …I mean, we, have a swamp cooler. And it's June. Summers up here in the desert are very hot, Steven but it will cool down come late October. Let's go inside and quench our thirst with something cold to drink. Do you like soda pop?"

"Yes sir," answered Steven, still not looking his grandfather in the face.

"That's good. First, a glass of ice water, though. If we don't drink enough water, we'll get dehydrated and come down with sunstroke or sun-poisoning. First a tall glass of water, Steven, then an ice-cold soda. How does that sound to you, Steven?"

"Okay," Steven said shyly. Steven had no idea what dehydrated, sunstroke, or sun-poisoning meant and was too intimidated to ask.

"We need to drink plenty of water every day," Henry explained. "Understand?"

"Yes, sir," said Steven, finally looking up at his grandad's face. "I understand."

This was Steven's first full look at the man people called his grandfather. He saw a large man wearing dark blue coveralls with a wrinkled face and gray hair on his head. His blue eyes twinkled, reflecting the setting desert sun.

"Great! Let's go, son," said Henry as he placed his hand on Steven's shoulder, guiding him to the house. Henry could see making the boy feel comfortable and want to talk would be a tall order.

As they began walking, Henry took his hand off Steven's shoulder and reached out for his grandson's hand. When the pair reached the two steps leading up to the wooden front porch, Stevens's eyes were scanning everything in his path. He noticed the porch's columns needed new paint and that the screen door was torn. His ears picked up the sounds of the porch's wooden floor squeaking beneath them. The front door looked like it had some of the same wrinkles that the old man he was supposed to call grandpa had.

Once inside the tiny house, Steven's eyes fell on a big stuffed chair that looked as if it took up the entire room. Next to the stuffed chair was a small wooden table with several pictures on it. Henry walked Steven to the table and let go of his hand.

"Have a seat and wait here for a moment, Steven, while I turn on the swamp cooler and grab each of us a nice, tall, ice-cold glass of water," said Henry.

Steven took a closer look at the photographs and noticed one picture was of him. The other photos showed three smiling people: a little girl and an older lady, both wearing fancy dresses standing beside a man who looked like his grandfather but without the wrinkles and gray hair.

The whirl of the swamp-cooler motor started, startling Steven, breaking his infatuation with the photographs. He turned to have a look at the rest of the room and noticed an old potbelly stove in the corner, something he was familiar with from some of the homes he lived at in Ohio. Against the far wall was a television set with rabbit ears antennae and a record player on top.

Beyond the stuffed chair, Steven saw a small table with two chairs around it. This is where grandfather must eat, he thought. The kitchen sink was behind that but could not be seen from all the dishes stacked on the countertop. The wallpaper on all four walls was torn and tattered, exposing older wallpaper behind it.

Turning, Steven noticed his grandfather standing in the hallway, staring at him. Henry walked to the kitchen, opened the refrigerator and pulled out a jug of water. He rinsed two glasses, filled them with ice cubes, and brought them and the jug of water to the table where Steven sat.

Pouring the water, Henry said, "Here you go, son. Drink up and then I'll show you around. It's getting late and it'll be dark soon so showing you around the outside will have to wait until tomorrow."

"Yes sir," said Steven, before drinking his glass of water.

"You don't need to call me 'Sir,' Steven. I'm your grandpa," explained Henry. "Understand?"

"Yes sir," Steven answered, finishing his water.

"One more glass of water, Steven, and then I'll get you a cold pop. Are you hungry, son?" asked Henry.

"No sir," said Steven.

"When was the last time you ate, Steven?" Henry asked.

"I ate dinner on the train, sir," said Steven.

"What did you have for dinner, Steven," asked Henry.

"Chicken, rice, and broccoli," Steven answered.

"How was it? Did it taste good?" Henry asked.

"It was okay," said Steven.

"Tomorrow, we'll sit down and make a list of the things you like to eat so I know what to buy for you when we go to the grocery store," said Henry.

Steven nodded his head. After drinking his second glass of water, Henry brought his grandson an ice-cold bottle of Coca-Cola. After a few sips of his Coke, Henry said to Steven, "This way, Steven, come with me."

Extending his arm and hand toward his grandson, Henry signaled for Steven to follow, and then walked the boy through the hallway to a door that opened to an exceedingly small room with one small bed and a chair in it.

"This is your room," Henry said. "When we're in town together tomorrow, I'll take you to a second-hand store and have you pick out a table for yourself and some books too. There's a small bookshelf in the garage we can clean up and bring in here for you in the morning. Do you like reading, Steven?"

"Yes, sir. I like Superman comic books," Steven said, finally beginning to let his guard down and open up.

"Then that's what we'll do," said Henry.

"Yes, sir," answered Steven.

Steven went back and took his seat at the table with the photographs on it to finish drinking his pop while Henry brought Steven's suitcase into the bedroom. When he returned to the living room, he noticed his grandson again staring intently at the photos. Neither said a word while Steven drank his soda.

"It's getting late and almost time for bed," said Henry. "Are you sure you're not hungry? I can make you a tuna sandwich on toast before you go to sleep. I understand that's your favorite."

Steven's eyes lit up and a wide smile came across his face. Learning that his grandfather knew what his favorite sandwich was made him feel special. But he wasn't hungry.

"Can I have the sandwich tomorrow, sir? I'm not hungry," asked Steven.

"You can call me 'Grandpa,' if you'd like, and yes, you can have a tuna sandwich on toast tomorrow for lunch," said Henry. "Finish up your soda, and then it's time to go into the bathroom, brush your teeth, and wash-up for bed. I brought your suitcase into your bedroom for you and there's a brand new toothbrush waiting on you on the bathroom counter inside a cup beside the paste."

"Yes sir," said Steven, who gulped down the last of the pop and then went into the bathroom and did as his grandpa instructed.

When Steven went into his bedroom, he noticed a new pair of pajamas on the bed, changed into them, and climbed into bed without turning off the bedroom light. Moving from home to home so often, whenever Steven woke up in the middle of the night, he often did not know where he was. Seeing the room made him remember.

Henry waited in the front room, expecting for the boy to come and say, "good night" before hopping into bed. After a several minutes passed, he decided to check on Steven. Henry sat down on Steven's bed and the two just looked at one another without either of them saying a word for several awkward moments.

Then Henry said, "Steven, I love you. This is home now. You're not going to be moved anywhere; you're here to stay. Do you understand?"

"Yes sir," answered Steven.

"OK. Time to turn off the light and go to sleep; we have a lot planned for tomorrow. Good night, Steven," said Henry.

"Sir," said Steven, just as Henry neared the doorway. "Is it OK if you leave the light on please?"

After a brief pause, Henry said, "Yes, for tonight."

"Thank you, sir," said Steven.

Nodding, Henry turned to walk out of the room when he heard Steven once again say, "Sir." When Henry turned back around, Steven said, "Thank you, sir, I mean, grandpa. I love you. Good night," and then the boy closed his eyes and went to sleep.

Choking back tears, Henry walked out of the room, shutting the door behind him, and leaving the light on. He went to sit where he always sat for the evening, in that big, old, stuffed chair. He usually turned on the TV set and fell asleep watching it, but tonight he grabbed a box of photographs from the bookshelf instead.

The first picture he looked at was of another small child – his daughter, Ashley, when she too was 6 years old, the same age as Steven now. Ashley was standing on the seashore holding a seashell. This evening was the first time in many, many years Henry looked at pictures of Ashley.

Though the photographs were of happy memories, Henry was conflicted because they reminded him of his loneliness living without his daughter and his wife. Henry thought about how much Ashley and Steven resembled one another. Steven had blond hair and blue eyes, just like Ashley.

He reminisced how Ashley's hair was always so pretty with the wind blowing through it while she was playing in sand down by the sea. He recalled the day Ashley collected seashells and made them into a necklace. He thought about the day she wore them with the beautiful white dress her mother made for her. Though Ashley looked so much like her mother, she was so much a daddy's girl! Henry began questioning what made Ashley decide to run away.

Henry felt like a shellfish; one day full of life and the next only an empty shell washed up on the shore. Henry moved to Mojave to get away from the sea and its memories, and now, with Steven in his life, these memories were returning. Deciding to call it a day, Henry placed the photographs back into the box and went to bed.

As he passed by Steven's room he stopped, quietly opened the door, looked in at his sleeping grandson and saw what just may bring a new meaning to his life. This time, he thought to himself, he just may have a fresh start that will put life back into the shell of an old man.

Ashley left home in 1948 when she was 17. She left a home full of love to rebel against what she considered a caged life; she felt trapped living in the small town of Cambria. Henry was extremely strict and protective of her. She found a boyfriend, which Henry did not approve of, and ended up running off with him.

From there, her life went downhill, and as much as Ashley missed her family, she felt too guilty to return home. She had called home a few times, never saying a word when her mom or dad answered, only listening to their voice, but the calls ended as her life continued to plummet.

When Ashley's boyfriend abandoned her, she began living on the street, selling her body to make a living and a bottle of Jack Daniels whiskey to drown her pain. How she found her way to

Ohio, no one seems to know, but there she found herself pregnant by the first real love she had since leaving home.

Falling in love with a good man helped her begin putting her life in order after several long years of unhappiness. She was clean and sober for over a year when she died giving birth to Steven. She was only 20 years old when she died in 1951, leaving her newborn without a mother. Steven's father disappeared as soon as he learned Ashley was pregnant.

Henry felt guilty about his daughter's leaving and never forgave himself for it. He had only felt love in his heart for his beautiful Ashley, and that love seemed to have driven her away. The empty nest he now lived in just may be filled with joy by his newfound grandson.

Chapter 2

A New Beginning

Morning came to the Mojave Desert as it would usually, with the sun shining brightly through Henry's window. Henry's morning routine consisted of waking up at sunrise, getting dressed, fueling his body with a cup of black coffee, and then going outside and walking to the garage where his old, green World War II Army Jeep purchased at auction was parked.

After loading mining tools he checked the belts, fluids, and tire pressure, and then filled up water bags to load on the passenger seat's floorboard. Henry always stopped at the corner diner for breakfast and company. Mornings at the diner were the only time Henry was around other people, forgetting about his loneliness.

The waitress, Claire, a twenty-something local gal that worked at the diner since she was in high school, always greeted Henry with a warm smile, asked about his plans for the day, which she knew, and then asked, "What'll it be today, Henry? The usual?" Henry's "usual" was black coffee, orange juice, two fried eggs, hash browns, bacon, and two pieces of toast topped with butter and strawberry jam.

On some days, Henry sat in a booth beside a few other regular customers, talking about current events. World War II ended nearly a decade ago, the Korean War armistice was signed just a few years back, and the Cold War between the US and Soviet Union was in its early throes. World-ending atomic warfare concerned everyone. Building bomb shelters was all the rage.

On most days, when Henry was feeling especially melancholy, he'd sit alone, head down, at the end of the counter. Claire sensed Henry's sadness on these occasions and would spend a few extra minutes talking with him, attempting to lift his spirits.

"I've got a hunch that today's the day that you strike it rich," Claire would always say with a warm smile and soft laugh.

"I never count my chickens before the eggs hatch," Henry always responded with a smile.

"If you do strike it rich today, Henry, don't forget about me!" Claire would reply.

"Honey, when I strike it rich, you're at the top of my list," was Henry's standard reply.

From there, a moment of small talk would ensue, followed by Claire handing Henry a copy of the morning edition of the Mojave Times tucked away under the counter, bought and saved just for him, and then she'd smile and walk away, going back to work, leaving Henry in peace with the morning newspaper until she brought his breakfast.

From time to time, when Claire placed the food on the counter, she would whisper to Henry, "Today's meal is on the house. Good luck out there today."

On these days, Henry left Claire double the normal tip before leaving the diner for the 45-minute ride to his mine located deep in the back hills.

This day at home before driving to the diner felt a bit different, compared to other than the cup of coffee, was different. Henry silently sat in his chair, drinking his coffee, waiting for Steven to wake up. After his coffee, excited about the new beginning, he decided to wait no longer and instead wake up the boy himself.

He walked to Steven's room, opened the door, and noticed the made bed was empty. Steven must be in the bathroom, he thought, but after a look there, he found it also empty. Fear and panic crossed Henry's mind. The boy must have gotten up in the middle of the night and ran off, just like his Ashley had many years before.

"No God! Not again! Please, NO!" Henry cried out. Heart pounding and beginning to sweat, he hollered even louder, "Steven!"

From the front porch, Henry heard Steven's soft voice reply, "Here I am, sir."

Steven was sitting on an old chair he found in the yard and brought onto the porch, looking at the sunrise. Henry went outside, saw the boy, exhaled, and gave the boy a tight hug.

"Good morning, Steven. You scared me. I panicked when I couldn't find you in the house. How long have you been out here?" asked Henry.

"I don't know. I can't tell the time, precisely," Steven replied. "But I know the stars were going away and the sky was just beginning to get light when I came out here. I didn't want to wake you up, sir. I hope it's okay that I brought this chair onto the porch. Am I in trouble?"

"Trouble? Why would you be in trouble, Steven? You didn't do anything wrong," explained Henry.

"I would get in trouble the last place I lived if I did something like this," said Steven.

"Like what, Steven?" Henry asked.

"Grab a chair from one place and move it to another without permission," Steven explained.

"Son, you're home now. This is your home. That chair you're sitting in belongs to both of us. You can place it anywhere you want to sit," said Henry. "Go into your room, put your shoes and socks on, and come back here and see me," said Henry. "I've got a big surprise for you. It's something special that I know you're going to love."

Steven got up off the chair, on his feet, and did as his grandfather told him. Once back outside, he wore an ear-to-ear smile, anticipating something good was about to happen. Henry led his grandson into the garage where his Jeep was parked waiting for its morning drive to the diner and then to the mine, but today was different. Today the Jeep was hiding a new boy's bicycle in front of it.

When Steven saw the bike, his eyes lit up; he never had a new bike before, just old bikes he shared with the other children in foster care. Henry lifted the blue bicycle with black handlebars with grips and a bell, and carried it outside to the front of the garage. Steven said, "Thank you, grandpa! I love you!" jumped right on, and down the driveway he went, ringing the bell over and over and over again!

Henry's wrinkled face now had a few more wrinkles on it from his large smile. The moment reminded him of the day Ashley got her first bike. It filled Henry's heart with joy seeing a child light up after receiving a new toy, but even better when that child was his grandson.

After watching Steven ride for about 15 minutes, Henry asked Steven if he was hungry for breakfast. Henry wanted to make breakfast for Steven like he always made breakfast for his wife and daughter in Cambria, but he wanted to take Steven to the diner and introduce him to his friends, and then to the local thrift store to buy a chair for his room, and then the market to buy food and Superman comic books. Making breakfast at home for Steven would have to wait for tomorrow.

Henry and Steven sat at the counter. Claire was looking forward to this morning; Henry made a point of updating her each time he received news on Steven. Yesterday at breakfast, Henry was an anxious nervous wreck knowing his grandson was set to arrive later that day.

Today was the first time Claire had ever seen Henry upbeat, smiling, and happy. "Looks like today's the day you finally struck gold, Henry!" Claire said with a warm smile and soft laugh. "Who do we have here?"

"Good morning, Claire! This here is my pot of gold, my grandson, Steven!" said Henry with a song in his voice and bounce in his step as he walked to the counter stool. "I'll have the usual. In fact, make it two! But substitute the coffee for milk for my boy."

Claire ordered the cook, walked back to Henry and Steven, placed a cold glass of milk in front of the boy, leaned in toward Henry and with a tear flowing down her cheek whispered, "Breakfast is on the house today, Henry." Then she smiled at Steven and went back to work.

"Why was that lady crying, grandpa?" Steven asked, noticing tears flowing down Henry's cheeks too. "Why are you crying, grandpa?"

"Because you're here, Steven; because you're here," Henry said softly, softly patting Steven on his head.

After breakfast, Henry took Steven to shopping and bought him everything he had promised. This day there was no mining, only Henry spending all day getting to know his grandson. It was Steven's day today.

Chapter 3
Returning to the Past to Begin a New Future

It is now the year 1958. A year has passed since Steven came to live with his grandfather. Henry and Steven have bonded well. Steven calls Henry "grandpa" every time, and no longer "sir." Henry has decided that the sparsely populated, desolate, harsh, and unbearably hot Mojave Desert is no place to raise a 7-year-old boy.

The time had come for Henry to leave Mojave and return to Cambria. The seaside community had been Henry's real home all along. He left to run away from his past; Mojave was an escape from the aching memories of the death of his wife and the loss of his daughter. Steven has given Henry the will to return.

Henry knew replacing his wife and daughter was impossible, but for Steven, he had something that echoed fond memories, and he was not going to throw it away in the desert town of Mojave. He still owned the house on the bluff in Cambria and it had been sitting empty for long enough.

Henry showed Steven pictures of the sea. Steven has never seen the ocean before. He also let Steven look at pictures of the house where his mom was raised and pictures of his mother on the seashore below when she was his age. Henry told Steven stories of his childhood days growing up in Cambria and how his dad – Steven's great-grandfather – made money mining in the pine-covered hills just outside of town.

When Henry's father sold his mines, he invested in land around Cambria and began raising dairy cattle. When Henry's dad died, he left Henry with a fortune. He had always dreamed of sharing that fortune with his daughter but had given up on that idea years ago when his Ashley left and never returned. She had been gone for far too long, and he did not think she would ever return.

Now, Ashley had returned to this child. Ashley may be gone forever, but she has been reborn in this child. Henry now had someone to leave his money to and someone to love again.

Henry sold all he owned in Mojave. After packing their personal items in the car it was time to leave for their new home, where they would experience the beauty of the sea. Leaving Mojave was not heartbreaking since it had only been a place to hide from the past. Henry and Steven loaded into the '49 Plymouth and made one last stop at the diner for old-time sake, and to bid a fond farewell to Claire.

"Looks like today is your lucky day; the day you've struck gold," Henry said to Claire. "You're investment has paid off."

"How so? You're leaving, Henry, and I feel like I'm losing a part of me," Claire said, choking back tears.

"Stick out your hands and close your eyes," said Henry, placing an 8"x5" envelope in Claire's hands.

"I can't take this," said Claire. "You need your money to take care of Steven and get things in order in Cambria. You told me that the old house needs a lot of work."

"Don't count your chickens before the eggs hatch," said Henry.

Confused, Claire peeked inside the envelope and saw that it did not contain cash but keys and paperwork. "What is this?" she asked.

"The keys and title to my, I mean, your new home and your new Jeep," Henry answered. "Thank you for all your kindness over the years. Your company and conversation were the one sure spot of happiness I could always count on these past few years."

Tears flowing, Claire asked, "The usual?"

"Yes," said Henry, now also crying. "The usual."

This time, Steven did not ask his grandfather why Claire was crying. He knew why. And he knew why his grandfather was crying too. Grandpa cooked breakfast for Steven every weekday morning before school. On weekends, they went to the diner, always sitting at the counter, and Claire would always spend time with them, asking Steven about his new life and how school was going. Steven loved Claire and knew he would probably never see her again. This thought made Steven cry too.

"Breakfast is on the house," Claire said with tears flowing down her cheeks as she placed their plates in front of them before turning and walking away to the back of the restaurant, out of sight, where she remained until Steven and Henry finished eating. Claire did not like goodbyes, so she stayed in the back until Henry and Steven left the diner.

Their drive to Cambria took them across the Tehachapi Mountains to Bakersfield, where they turned west and drove through the oil fields and rolling hills until they reached the Pacific Ocean. Neither said much during the ride. Henry's mind was preoccupied with the tasks before him upon arrival in Cambria. Steven thought about finally the seeing the ocean and playing in the waves.

"Are you okay, grandpa?" Steven asked.

"Yes. Why do you ask?" Henry inquired.

"You're awful quiet. I thought maybe something is wrong? Did I do something wrong, grandpa?" Steven asked.

"Not all at, Steven," Henry replied.

"Then why so quiet?" said Steven.

"You're not talking either, Steven," said Henry. "What's on your mind? What are you thinking about?"

"I miss Claire," said Steven. "Do you think we'll see here again someday?"

"Perhaps," Henry said. "We never know what the future may bring."

"What are you thinking about, Grandpa?" Steven asked.

"I'm thinking about all the work we have before us and how happy I am that we're going to be living by the sea. I have a lot of great memories living by the sea and I'm looking forward to making more great memories there with you," said Henry.

After driving several hours, they finally reached Highway 101 in Paso Robles. Now it was down to only minutes and they would be home! The refreshing, cool, salty air hit Steven as soon as the car crested the foothills and the sea was in view.

"What's that smell, grandpa?" Steven asked.

"That's the smell of the sea and fresh ocean air," said Henry. "Do you like it?"

"Yes," Steven answered. "And the air, it's so cool. Does it get hot here, grandpa."

"Not like the desert, Steven," said Henry. "It gets warm here when the wind blows in from the east. It's all called an off-shore flow. But it never gets hot. Do you like that too?"

"Yes," Steven answered. "I think I like the sea way better than the desert already."

"Me too, Steven. Me too," said Henry, smiling.

"Grandpa?" said Steven.

"Yes, Steven," said Henry.

"I love you, grandpa," said Steven. "Thank you for bringing me to live by the sea."

"I love you too, Steven," said Henry.

Steven was silent the final few minutes of the drive, in awe and enamored by the new scenery, the new smells, and the new town. Henry was unable to recall the last time he was this happy.

On their first night in Cambria, Steven and his grandfather stayed at the Seaside Inn, owned by Carol Hanson. Carol had known Henry for years and was a particularly good friend of Henry's deceased wife, Victoria. Carol lost her husband only a year ago and was left to tend the Inn by herself. Carol was beyond herself, unable to contain her jubilation when she saw Henry and Steven.

"Henry! Oh my God, Henry!" screamed Carol, running toward him, arms spread wide for a hug and sobbing. "Oh, it's soooooooo good to see you! Welcome home, Henry! Welcome home!"

Henry and Carol embraced, Carol refusing to let go for nearly a minute, the two rocking back and forth. After breaking the hug, Carol stepped back, sighed, looked at Steven and said, "And this handsome young man must be Steven. Welcome home, Steven. It's so good to finally meet you. I've heard so much about you. I have a big surprise for you."

Carol led Steven and Henry to a booth inside the Inn's dining area where there were two wrapped gifts sitting on the table. Inside one box were several comic books, including the latest issue of Superman. Inside the second box were swimming trunks, a towel, and a few books. One book was about seashells, another about local marine life, and one taught how to build sand castles.

"Carol, how much do I owe you for all this," said Henry.

"Nonsense!" Carol replied. "You and Steven are family. Now the two of you take a seat and I'll be right back with some food."

After eating, Carol led them to their room. While Steven thumbed through his books, she and Henry sat on the patio reminiscing about old times for nearly an hour. It sure was good to be home again, Henry was thinking, as he looked out at the sea. Excited about being near the ocean, Steven changed into his brand new swimming trunks and with towel in hand asked if he could go down to the beach below. Henry took him by the hand and off they went, walking the small trail next to the Inn down along the green-covered bluff leading to the sandy beach below.

The sound of the waves and the seagulls were making Henry's heart pound. The hands of time had turned back the clock. In his mind, it was as if it was the 1930s and he was holding Ashley's hand, looking at the sea together. Henry and Ashley had walked the same trail many times. The feelings racing through Henry were almost unbearable. Tears rolled down his face as he took the handkerchief from his shirt pocket and wiped them away.

"Why are you crying grandpa?" Steven asked.

Henry picked up Steven and held him close. "Because I'm happy that you're here with me," said Henry. Pointing to the beach, he then said, "Let's go find seashells."

He put Steven down and they continued walking down the trail. They both took off their shoes when they reached the beach. Steven giggled when he felt sand between his toes and asked permission to go to the water's edge and feel the sea on his feet and legs. Laughing, Steven hopped up and down in the sea foam as it lapped the shore. When the water receded, he looked down and saw his first seashell. His little face beamed with happiness!

"Look, grandpa! A seashell!" he shouted.

"Look at that," said Henry. "Your first seashell! It's a real looker, and a keeper too! You'll need to show that to Carol."

Both grandfather and grandson walked along the beach until they came across a cave that went back about 10 feet into the cliff's bank. Next, they came upon a tide pool at the front of the cliff and Steven saw his first sea creatures, including a star fish. After an hour on the beach, it was time for them to walk back up to the road get back to Inn in time for dinner. Tomorrow would be another big day.

Before putting Steven into bed, Henry and his grandson stepped out onto the front porch and watched the sun drop below the ocean's horizon in one of the prettiest sunsets Henry had seen in a long, long time. The sunsets in the Mojave Desert were always great, but the sunsets setting on the sea were something to behold.

Once Steven was asleep, Carol and Henry talked about Henry's return home. Carol was caught with disbelief when Henry left Cambria, shutting the door to the past, trying to run away from the pain of losing his wife and the apparent guilt of causing his daughter to run away.

Carol brought Henry up to date on the town's goings-on since he left and asked him when he was planning to move back into his empty house on the bluff. Since the house sat vacant for so long and certainly needed repairing, she was surprised to learn that he planned on moving in in a few days. They talked for hours, though it seemed like minutes. It was now almost midnight. Henry had a big day before him tomorrow so he thanked Carol for her company, excused himself, and went to bed.

After a good night's sleep, Henry got up and woke up Steven. The big day was here! One part of Henry could not wait to return home and the other part was anguished over the reason he left in the first place. Driving down Main Street, Henry and Steven passed by shops that Henry and his wife shopped at often. Henry felt like he was indeed home. He was overcome with good feelings; this was certainly the right place to be.

Mr. Higgins was standing in front of the old miner's supply store that was now Higgins' Antiques. With its old, weathered boards on the front and the wooden porch with hanging lanterns wired for electric lights, the front of the building still looked just like it did when Henry was last here. The old, wooden miner's wheelbarrow with its steel front wheel, filled with flowers, still sat alongside the building placed in the middle of a very green lawn. Beside the wheelbarrow was the wishing well. Henry used to lift Ashley so she could throw in a penny for good luck.

Looking to the other side of the street was Glen Cliff's Ice Cream. It was a hunt for Henry's family on a Friday night, along with all of Henry's friends. It had been like a meeting place to talk about anything and everything that happened to anyone in Cambria. The car seemed to be running on its own as it pulled over to the curb in front of the ice cream store. Henry just sat there for a minute and then said, "How about some ice cream, Steven? Are you up for an ice cream cone?"

Steven replied, "I sure am!"

"What kind do you want?" asked Henry.

"I'll take strawberry please," Steven said.

"Let's make that strawberry ice cream a double-dipped cone!" laughed Henry.

Lost in the moment, Henry stood for a minute or two watching Steven lick on the strawberry ice cream cone. Afterward, he took Steven's hand and they walked back to the car. It was time to get down to the electric company and have the lights turned on at the old house, and then on to the water and gas companies. Then it was the final stop, the one he had been waiting on: his return to the house.

Henry was conflicted. Part of him did not look forward to returning to his old home. He feared bringing back too many bad memories. He was unsure if the good memories would outweigh the bad ones. The old '49 Plymouth had driven down this road many times; a road meandering past green fields with grazing cattle hemmed in by wire fences. On a clear day, one could see for miles from this road, and if you knew where to look, one could see Henry's house peeking out from among the pines covering the top of the bluff.

The road through the pine trees leading to Henry's blue and white Victorian house went from paved to dirt about one-quarter mile from the driveway. The view of the sea from this spot was magnificent! The closer they were to the house, the tenser Henry became. He began sweating as the car rounded the final curve leading to the driveway. There it was. Henry's old home and now Steven's new home. Henry silently told himself to be emotionally strong for Steven's sake.

The picket fence in the front yard used to be white and the rose bushes once covered most of it, but the roses were all dead by now except for a few bushes that seemed to have survived on their own without any care from anyone. The white fence was not very white anymore; it missed the care of Henry's paintbrush. But, that would all change now because Henry was home.

"There it is, Steven," said Henry. "Our new home. What do you think?"

"Wow! It's a lot bigger than our home in Mojave. I can't wait to see what it looks like inside!" said Steven. "Let's go, grandpa! Let's go have a look!"

Henry did not know if he was up to entering the old home at all. Steven was so excited. He opened his car door, exited, and ran around to Henry's side as soon as Henry turned off the motor. Steven grabbed the door handle, opened the driver's door, and said, "Come on, grandpa, let's go inside! Hurry!"

"What a difference one year makes," Henry said as he laughed.

Henry, fixated on the house, turned his head toward Steven. As soon as he saw his beaming face he placed his left leg on the ground outside the car. His right leg seemed to be stuck or just wasn't getting the orders from Henry's brain to move. Finally, his leg moved and Henry was standing outside the car. With one hand holding Steven's hand, they started their walk toward the house.

The porch swing still hung by its chains on the front porch. Henry remembered how he and Victoria would sit, side-by-side, Victoria's head resting on his shoulders, not saying a word to one another, swinging gently, admiring the ocean view through the pine forest and the green pastures, enjoying the sea's cool breeze.

Victoria used to love sitting on the porch watching Henry work in the yard, and Henry loved the work. He always had the prettiest roses of so many different colors. Before Ashley left the house for good, she planted a few rose bushes alongside Henry. Two of the bushes Ashley planted were among the few that survived during Henry's absence. They were in bad shape but alive. Henry knew he just had to save them; they brought back many good memories. When the sun rose from behind the house, it would cast its rays on the ocean below. This was Henry's signal to go inside and begin cooking breakfast. Henry loved to cook, and that was always okay with Victoria because she loved his cooking.

The fancy screen door Henry built for Victoria as a Christmas present was still in good shape. He loved working in his shop that was attached to the garage that stood beside the house. His wrinkled hand, darkened from the desert sun, reached out to take hold of the screen door's handle. The hinges creaked from lack of oil when the door opened. The solid oak front door with the carving of a guardian angel complemented the entire view. Henry used to tell Ashley that the angel watched over her dad and mom.

Henry's hand trembled when he inserted the key into the door lock. The front door's hinges squeaked too from lack of oil. Slowly, he pushed open the door. On the other side of the door was the entry hallway with the hall tree Henry hanged his coat and hat on. Other than being covered in a thick blanket of dust, the hall tree looked fine too.

A large brown spider had spun a web at the entryway to the living room. Henry grabbed an old brush lying atop a small table beside the hall tree and cleared away the web. Beyond the living room was the stairway leading to the second floor. A masterpiece in craftsmanship, the stairway added charm to the house.

The beautiful, oak steps and the solid oak handrail curved its way to the top. At the top of the stairs was a large, beveled glass window that sent rays of light looking like a rainbow across the ceiling at sunrise. Henry heard the sound of a truck arriving as he began walking into the living room.

It was Jay Burton from the water and power company. He and Steven went outside to meet Jay and walked him around to the electric meter where Jay removed and replaced the insulators from the back of the meter.

"Your power is on now, Henry," said Jay. "Welcome home. Looks like you've got your work cut out for you."

"Thank you, Jay. And yes I do," said Henry. "I'd like to introduce you to someone special. This is my grandson, Steven. Ashley's son."

"Beautiful boy, Henry," said Jay. "Where's Ashley? Around back?"

"Ashley is with God now," Henry said.

"I'm sorry to hear that," Jay said, looking down in sorrow.

After a brief silence, with a kind smile and firm handshake Jay said good bye, returned to his truck, waving as he drove away. Back in the house now, Henry looked around, took a deep breath, and told Steven it was time to get to work. Everything was covered in dust. Henry walked to the hall closet where the vacuum cleaner and dust cloths were always kept. He handed the dust cloths to his grandson and asked Steven to take them outside, shake the dust off them, and come back in and begin wiping the furniture.

"Whenever the rags become covered in dust, take them outside to the yard far away from the front door and shake them out," Henry instructed the boy. "And then come back in and pick up where you left off. We'll have the house dust free soon enough."

After Henry emptied the vacuum bag into the trash barrel sitting outside the house, he plugged in the vacuum and flipped on the start switch. The motor started, ejecting more dust. Running the vacuum exposed the wooden floor as the dust was sucked up into the vacuum.

While dusting, Steven knocked a picture off the coffee table, breaking the glass when it hit the floor. Henry turned off the vacuum, walked over to the picture and picked it up. It was a picture of Ashley.

"Who is that in the picture, grandpa," asked Steven.

"This is a photo of your mother when she was 16 years old," Henry answered. "This is one of the last photos ever taken of her."

Steven was mesmerized and stared intently at his mother's picture. He set back the picture after taking the glass, the way it was set before, Henry resumed his work, and vacuumed the floor. Though early summer, the cool ocean breeze kept the inside of house cold. The air temperature hit 62 degrees, a far cry from the triple digits of the Mojave Desert Steven and Henry lived in.

The natural gas used to heat the home had not been turned on yet, but the house had a great fireplace and firewood was still neatly stacked outside. Henry decided to take a break from vacuuming the floor and instead clean the inside of the empty fireplace. He had Steven dust the hearth, mantle, and irons, and then the two of them walked outside the house and brought in an armload of wood.

"Do you know how to start a fireplace fire, Steven?" Henry asked.

When Steven shook his head, Henry instructed him to watch closely. Henry opened the flue and placed the paper he found in the waste can on the log holder. He placed kindling on top of that, followed by thin branches. The two small logs across the top of that pointed out to Steven that the edges of the logs rested on the edge of the log holder, providing a few inches of space between the logs and kindling.

"All this wood is extremely dry," said Henry. "We'll have a nice, warm fire in no time."

Henry lit a match and set the edges of the waste paper on fire, which quickly ignited the kindling and immediately set the thin branches ablaze. The logs caught fire instantly. The fireplace had been one of Henry's favorite places to sit on a damp, frigid evening with his wife in his arms. Now the fire was lit for heat and not for the warmth he once found in his lovely wife, Victoria.

Back to work dusting, Steven and Henry cleaned all the light fixtures so the lights could be turned on in the living room. Next was the furniture. Though Henry covered all the furniture with sheets before he left, he had been gone so long that dust filtered through them.

He started with the nine-foot-long couch placed to the right of the fireplace. Victoria had picked out the baby blue-colored couch a few years before she died. It was a beautiful couch that complemented the living room. Henry and Victoria sat silently on the couch together looking out the picture window, admiring the pine trees.

There was a love seat opposite the couch at the other side of the room placed facing a window looking out to the ocean. This was Victoria's favorite view. The large window with its beveled glass edges looked like a picture frame, framing the sunset as it dipped below the sea.

Henry and Steven worked until noon and took a lunch break eating sandwiches Carol made and packed for them. Then it was back to work until suppertime, which they would eat at the Inn where they would once again spend the night. Tomorrow night they would finally sleep at home sweet home.

When they arrived at the Inn covered in dust and dirt, Carol commented, "I see two hungry men after a hard day's work.

How about getting cleaned up real nice and coming over to my place for a hot meal. Let's say 45 minutes."

It was an offer they could not refuse. They were both hungry enough to eat a horse! Time cleaning the old home had gone by so fast that they had both forgotten just how hungry they were.

"Carol reminds me of Claire," said Steven, which made Henry chuckle.

"Me too," said Henry. "And the meal Carol is feeding us will also be on the house."

"We're lucky, Grandpa," added Steven.

"You have no idea how lucky we are," Henry said. "With you in my life, I feel like the luckiest man on the face of God's earth."

After cleaning up, they walked to Carol's place, where she was waiting for them with a hot meal consisting of pork chops and applesauce, mashed potatoes with gravy, broccoli topped with cheddar cheese, and fresh-baked bread rolls and butter.

All in all, Henry and Steven made an evening out of it, spending over two hours at Carol's house. On their way out, Carol told Henry that she arranged for someone to mind the Inn tomorrow to free her up so she could tag along and help them clean the house. Henry was not going to turn down any offer of help; they could use all the help that they could get.

Morning came so fast. Tired from working hard the day before, Steven and Henry slept well. At 7am, Carol called their room letting them know that breakfast will be ready in 15 minutes. After eating, Carol surprised Henry with several bags of groceries and a house-warming gift she purchased the day before.

"Carol, you really should not be spending money on us. I have more than enough to buy everything Steven and I need," said Henry.

"Just like Victoria always said about you, you're a very cheerful giver but need to learn how to be a grateful receiver," said Carol sternly. "Now that will be enough of that. I know that Victoria is looking down on us from heaven and appreciates my looking out for you. How about just smiling and saying 'Thank you, Carol.'"

"Thank you, Carol," said a grinning Henry.

"Now, was that so difficult?" said Carol, who turned her attention toward Steven, adding, "Your grandpa is a wonderful man and you should do your best to be just like him when you grow up, all except not willing to take help from others. There's nothing wrong with accepting help."

This morning's weather was different from yesterday. Coastal low clouds and fog, known as a marine layer, set in overnight. Steven was mesmerized by the sight. Carol explained to the boy that the weather phenomenon is called "June Gloom" and would lift and retreat back over the ocean by 10 or 11 am when clear blue skies would prevail. Low visibility made for a slow drive. The house was obscured by the fog; only the rooftop, four chimneys, and four turrets were visible.

"The low clouds and fog are like the tide," Carol explained to Steven. "They'll roll back out to sea soon enough."

Carol cleaned the kitchen while Henry and Steven finished getting the living and dining rooms back in tip-top shape. The kitchen cabinets were still full of dishes that needed to be removed, washed, dried, and placed back into the cabinets. By noon, nearly completely clean, the downstairs was beginning to look livable again.

The first task after lunch was tackling the staircase and then the second-floor bedrooms and bathrooms. The first bedroom Steven and Henry cleaned was the room where Victoria died. She had been in so much pain before she passed away that she could not leave the bedroom the final weeks of her life unless Henry carried her down the stairs.

Victoria could not be moved at all the few days before she died because of the pain, so Henry sat next to her bed, reading to her and caring for her every need until the end. Henry just could not stay in the house after she was buried, and that is when he moved to Mojave. Now, he was standing at the door looking at the very bed Victoria had died in. This would be one bed that Henry would not be sleeping in; the guest room would now be Henry's bedroom.

The gas company arrived mid-afternoon and cleaned the old furnace that heated the water for the home's steam heaters. Nearly the entire house had been cleaned by day's end.

Evening came and it was time to take Carol back to the Inn, gather their belongings, check out of their room, and pay Carol, which proved difficult because Carol did not want to accept Henry's money. After briefly friendly bickering, Henry placed cash on the counter, grabbed Steven's hand, thanked Carol for the meals, food, and help, and began walking out of the Inn for the drive home when Carol called him back.

"Not, so fast, Mr. Benson," said Carol. "One more thing."

"What now?" Henry asked.

"I'm not taking this money," she said. "But Steven will. I expect to see you and Steven in a few days, and we're going to the bank together because I'm using this money to open a savings account for your grandson."

Henry did not say a word. He knew arguing would be futile. Instead, he grabbed Steven by the hand and walked him to the car for the drive home. When Henry got to the car, he noticed Carol had someone surreptitiously place new bedding and pillows in the back seat when he wasn't looking. Atop the bedding was an envelope with a card inside. The card read, "Welcome Home!" Inside was a handwritten note from Carol telling Henry how wonderful it was to have him back in town and not to forget that she was only a phone call away if he needed anything.

Henry read the card aloud to Steven. "People around here really love you, grandpa," Steven said.

Henry nodded his head in agreement, started the car, and the two began to drive up the hill to begin their new life in an old home.

Chapter 4

The Letter

Steven's bedroom was next to the guest room where Henry was sleeping. After changing the bedding with the new sheets and blankets Carol gave them, it was time to wash up and go to bed. Tomorrow would soon be here and there was still plenty of work left to put the house back the way it belonged.

The painters Henry hired arrived bright and early. They were tasked with replacing wallpaper as well. The new paint eliminated the old smell that their house now had. All the curtains needed to be replaced too. Age had caused its share of damage to the curtains that Victoria had made herself. It would be hard to see them go but there was not any choice in the matter. Henry watched his wife sit for hours making those curtains, and now in minutes they would all be gone.

While the painters were busy inside the house, Henry and Steven worked outside cleaning windows before repairing and sanding the fence in front of the property. The painters would repaint the fence and home's exterior tomorrow while Henry and Steven went into town to buy new curtains. Before the day ended, the telephone service was turned on. Henry called the nursery and ordered rose bushes to plant along the fence, replacing the old ones that died in his absence.

After a week of work, the old place just looked like it would look in its happier days. Next up was shoring up and clearing weeds along the trail leading down to the beach below. No one had walked that trail for a long time. Hard work did not bother Henry, even at his age. Working in the Mojave mine kept him in good shape. Cleaning a home and repairing property was easy compared to mining.

While workers from the nursery were busy laying sod for the new lawn in the front and backyards, Henry and Steven began clearing the trail. The beach below was semi-private save for a small cottage that sat about 100 yards down from Henry's house.

This cottage was once owned by Henry's dad until he sold it to a friend who lived in New York City who used it as a vacation home a few months every year. Like Henry's house, the cottage too, Henry learned from Carol, had been vacant for several years.

A narrow path from the beach led to the cottage. The beach itself was inaccessible otherwise due to it being closed off by bluffs that stretched into the sea on either side. Years ago, locals referred to this section of the coastline as "Pirates Cove." Legend had it that pirates hid their ill-gotten loot and contraband in the cove. Some people believed that the ghosts of pirate ships could be seen anchored offshore on a moonlit night.

Before Henry was born, his dad hired workmen to cut the two-foot-wide trail down the bluff to the beach below. When Henry moved into his dad's old house with his new wife, Victoria, the trail did not have a handrail. Once Ashley was born, Henry had a rail installed the entire length of the trail. Henry would never let Ashley go near the trail alone until she was a teenager.

Ashley spent a lot of time collecting seashells on the beach; she had one of the best seashell collections and would often take 1st Place in Cambria's annual summer fair. Henry would stand for hours at the top of the bluff looking down on Ashley at play, her long blonde hair blowing in the ocean breeze while she walked across the sand looking for just the right shell to bring home. Now it would be Steven that would walk the beach and find treasures with Henry by his side.

By the end of the day the trail was in decent shape and it was time to go back to the house where the painters were loading up their things for the day. Tomorrow would be the first day Henry would receive mail at the house so he decided to clean the inside and outside of the old mailbox. When he began wiping it down, the 4x4 post the mailbox sat upon toppled over.

As he picked up the mailbox, its door opened and a letter fell out. The envelope was browned from age but had been protected from the weather inside the box. Addressed to Mr. and Mrs. Henry Benson, it had no return address. The postmark read March 17, 1954 – just over four-years ago. It had been mailed a few weeks after he moved to Mojave.

When Henry opened the envelope he could not believe his eyes. The letter, dated 1952, was from Ashley, the year after she died. So who mailed it? Henry knew he should be sitting down when he read the letter so he and Steven went back to the house. Once inside, Henry grabbed his glasses, took a seat, and began reading the letter from his daughter.

Steven noticed that his grandad looked concerned and asked, "What is it, granpa? Is it an important letter?"

Henry replied, "Just a letter I must read."

The letter read:

Dear mom and dad,

I'm so sorry for all these years. I'm so sorry for treating you the way I have. I always loved each of you so much and have wanted to come back home for oh so many years. I just could not bring myself home to see you in the condition that I found myself in for all these years.

Dad was right when he did not want me to see Bill. I was so wrong by running away with him. Just like dad had said so many times before, Bill was a bad person. It took a few years after I left to find that out. My eyes were so blind to the truth.

My life has been nothing but hell since I left. But this year, I'm trying to put it back together. Never has a day passed by without thoughts of you both. I found my way to the middle of nowhere and had no way to return. Bill had taught me how to drink and drinking became my downfall. He started treating me so badly that I found myself drinking more and more each day just to escape the pain of being with him.

I tried to leave him one day and he found me packing and beat me so badly that I was in bed for days. At that time, he told me if I tried it again he would kill me. The drinking only got worse; each day started feeling like years passing by with no comfort in knowing that the next day would only bring the same thing.

So many times I found myself picking up the phone to call, dialing the numbers and hearing your voice on the other end saying Hello, wanting so much to reply, but I just couldn't bring myself to do it. I wanted to come home so badly but there was not any way I wanted to bring into your lives what I now had become.

I was with Bill for about two years and the only way out this life was the day he died in a car wreck. I know it is wrong to be happy when someone dies, but I thought to myself that this would be a new beginning for me. No more beatings from Bill. The car accident ended all this drama. But it did not end the bottle I now had in my hands each day.

Without Bill I found myself without any money. The house that Bill and I rented was the only place I had been at and now they wanted me out for not paying the rent. Where was I to go? I know I would have liked to return home to be with the only ones I have ever loved, the two of you.

One of Bill's friends stepped into what I thought would be to help. He moved me in with him because I did not have a place to go. I thought for a while that he was just a nice guy, but I should have known better that being Bill's friend could only mean one thing, and that was not just being nice. He had replaced the empty bottles of alcohol with new ones and had put me on the streets to earn my keep.

This went on for several months until a girlfriend helped me leave. She had some money that her folks had sent her to return home and she took me with her. This was how I ended up in Ohio. It still took years to straighten up my life, but this year I feel I am ready to return home. I will be leaving soon.

Love,

Ashley

P.S. I'm so sorry to have caused you pain. Please forgive me.

Tears flowed down every wrinkle on Henry's face. He put the letter down. It was so hard to understand why the love of his life had to go through so much pain. If only he had known where she had been and brought her home. She must have written the letter but never mailed it for some reason.

Henry got up from the couch and went to the old trunk that he kept his important papers in. He grabbed the letter that was said to have been written by a friend of Ashley's in Ohio. This is how he had found out he had a grandson. This must have been the friend that Ashley was now talking about in her letter.

A letter mailed to him in Mojave from Bowling Green, Ohio, was from a lady that was Ashley's friend who wrote that she had been trying to find Henry for a few years. She explained in the letter that, after calling a few places in Cambria, she found someone that knew Henry and learned he had moved to

Mojave. In the letter, it told of Ashley giving birth and dying, leaving a baby boy that was placed in foster care.

After finding this out, Henry had written to Ohio's Department of Health and Welfare to find out if this were true. Records revealed that Steven was brought to them by someone claiming that the mother, named Ashley Benson, died giving birth. A driver's license with the name of Ashley Benson on it was also given to them.

Ohio remanded the lady into custody and required her to submit to a blood test to ensure the baby was not hers. Once cleared, she was released. The department researched records and could not locate documentation verifying that an Ashley Benson had died in Ohio. Because the father's identity was unknown, Steven was given Benson as his last name.

Chapter 5

Ashley Returns Home

It was now May 1961. Steven was 10, and Henry was 61. He and Henry had been happily living in Cambria for three years now. Steven spent most summer days at the beach. Today, he and Henry were going into town to eat pasta at Mustache Pete's Place – the best pasta and seafood restaurant in town.

After entering Mustache Pete's, they ran into Jack Hill, an old friend of Henry's – of course about everyone in town was an old friend of Henry's. Everyone in town knew everyone else in town. The only strangers were those passing through. Jack, like Henry, grew up in Cambria.

"Did you hear that the old cottage down a spell from your home sold?" Jack asked Henry.

"That's news to me, Jack," answered Henry. "Any idea who the buyer is?"

"All I know about the buyer is she is a younger woman, maybe 30 or so. Folks are saying she looks like a movie star the way she wears sunglasses and a scarf pulled around her head," said Jack. "I crossed paths with Gus, who works at water and power, and Gus tells me he saw her when she was down his way to have the water and power turned on. I also hear she hired a crew to clean up the place, too."

"Did Gus tell you her name?" Henry asked.

"I never did ask Gus her name," said Jack.

Henry went down to water and power after eating at Mustache Pete's Place and learned that his new neighbor's name was Kim Brooks. Gus, like most people in town, believed Kim Brooks, who made a point of concealing her face, was a pseudonym that this person, who must be someone important, used to ensure privacy.

Bringing the cottage up to living standards was going to require a lot of work since it had been vacant longer than Henry's home. It always looked so nice when Henry was a kid, and his dad owned it. When the people from New York bought it they had it repainted gray with white trim and the fence around the yard painted white. It looked surprisingly good when it was all finished. Since they never stayed there full-time, the place started going downhill. Henry knew it would be great to have a neighbor again.

A few days later, Henry noticed several cars driving by his house on their way to the cottage up the road. He figured they must be the work crew. Next, a fancy-looking red convertible sports car with the top down driven by a woman wearing sunglasses and a head scarf drove by. Henry and Steven got into the old Plymouth and went to the cottage to meet their new neighbor. After arriving at the cottage, they both climbed out of the car and walked up to where the woman was standing.

Henry said, "Hi! My name is Henry Benson, and this fine lookin' young man with me is my grandson, Steven. We live in the house you just passed by a few minutes ago."

"Hi neighbor. My name is Kim Brooks. It's nice to meet you," she said without taking off her sunglasses. "I'm delighted that you took the trouble to come down here to meet me."

"No trouble at all, Miss Brooks," Henry replied.

Kim explained that she was excited to be in Cambria and loved the ocean and walking on the beach, as she did as a child, and was so happy to be able to do it again. When Henry inquired where she grew up, Kim behaved as if she did not hear the question and instead said, "Well, it sure was nice meeting you, Mr. Benson, and you too Steven. I need to get inside and let my workers know what needs to be done first."

Before turning and walking away, Kim paused and took a long look at Steven, which Henry found peculiar. Henry figured that would be the last time he would see Kim in person. He too felt like Kim was someone trying to get away from people, so he planned on not bothering her again.

The next morning when Kim drove by Henry's house, Henry and Steven were sitting on the front porch. Kim, wearing headscarf and sunglasses, waved as she drove by. Later in the day when Steven was down at the beach, Kim came walking along.

"What-cha' doin', Steven," Kim asked.

"Collecting seashells, ma'am," Steven replied.

"You don't have to call me 'ma'am, Steven. You can call me Kim," she said.

"No ma'am. Grandpa said to always show respect by referring to adults as 'sir' and 'ma'am,'" Steven explained.

"Well, that sure is the decent thing to do. How 'bout calling me Miss Brooks or Miss Kim? Would Grandpa object to that?" she asked.

"I'll ask him," Steven said.

Kim, again wearing a headscarf and sunglasses, stayed with Steven for over an hour, collecting seashells. She told him how she, too used to collect seashells with her dad when she was a little girl and lived in a house not too far from the shore, just like he did.

"Where did you grow up?" Steven asked.

"My favorite seashells are pinkish in color. What about you?" she asked, instead of answering Steven's question.

"I like the bluish ones best," Steven answered.

Every time Steven asked Kim where she grew up or any other question about her childhood, Kim acted like she did not hear him and instead asked him another question.

Before Kim left the beach to go back home, she told Steven that she would help him collect seashells any time he wanted. Once

Kim left, Steven decided to climb back up the hill and tell his grandpa about what happened. Unbeknownst to Steven, Henry was watching them on the beach from the bluff. Henry thought to himself how he'd obviously been wrong about the woman wanting to be left alone in solitude, that maybe she liked to be around people, or at least children.

"Miss Brooks told me that I don't need to call her 'ma'am' but can call her by her first name, Kim, or Miss Kim, or Miss Brooks," Steven told his grandpa. "I told her that you have me call adults 'sir' or 'ma'am,' and she said she'd talk to you about it. Can I call her something other than 'ma'am,' grandpa? Can I?"

"I'll think about that, Steven. Maybe not just yet. Maybe after we get to know her a little better," Henry said. "Until then, it's 'ma'am.'"

The next day, the same thing happened when Steven was on the beach. Down came Kim, again wearing her movie star sunglasses and headscarf. Henry took notice and decided to walk down to the beach and join them. Though he and Kim talked for several hours, Henry was unable to learn any details about her life.

"Howdy. Mind if I join the two of you? Looks like you're having fun," said Henry.

"Of course not; the more the merrier," said Kim.

"I used to come down to this very beach with my daughter to collect seashells together when she was a little girl," commented Henry. "Did you collect seashells, too when you were a little girl, Kim?"

"I did! My dad and I would collect seashells together, just like you and your daughter," said Kim. "What's your daughter's name, Mr. Benson?"

"Ashley," answered Henry.

"What a beautiful name. I hope to meet her someday," said Kim. "Does she live with you? I don't think I've ever seen her around."

"That, unfortunately, is not possible. Ashely is in heaven," said Henry, with a forced smile.

"I'm sorry," said Kim.

"Where did you grow up, Ms. Brooks?" Henry asked.

"It sure is a nice day today," said Kim. "Seashells bring back so many wonderful memories. I miss my mom and dad."

"Where do they live now," Henry asked, hoping to gain insight into the life and background of his new neighbor. "Hopefully not too far away."

"I love the cool ocean breeze too," said Kim. "It's so refreshing."

Kim changed the subject whenever Henry asked a personal question. He could tell she really did not want to talk much about herself, so he stopped asking her about her life. She did answer one personal question. Noticing she did not wear a wedding ring, Henry asked about Mr. Brooks, and Kim divulged that she was not married before excusing herself to go back home.

"Well, I need to get going. I have a few things to tend to at home," said Kim. "See you both soon."

The next day, while Steven was in school, Kim stopped by Henry's house on her way to town to ask Henry if there was anything he needed that she could pick up for him. When Henry declined and thanked Kim for her concern, Kim asked if there was anything Steven might need.

"He's a very special boy," said Kim. "I enjoy spending time with him. I hope you don't mind. Collecting seashells on the beach with him brings back so many wonderful memories for me. Is there anything Steven needs that I can bring from town?"

"I think he's all set too, but thank you Miss Brooks," Henry said.

"Please, call me Kim, Mr. Benson. May I call you Henry?" asked Kim.

"Okay, Kim. And yes, Henry is just fine," Henry answered.

"I told Steven to call me Kim, but he said you require him to call adults 'sir' or 'ma'am.' Is that right?" Kim asked.

"Yes it is. He needs to show respect for his elders," Henry said.

"Steven is lucky to have you in his life, Henry," said Kim. "Perhaps one day soon I can become more than just a 'ma'am' in Steven's life. I often wish that I had a child; a little boy to call my own," she said, adding, "Tootle-loo, Henry," with a wave as she turned and walked back to her car.

Henry still did not know what Kim's face looked like because, once again, she was sporting sunglasses and a headscarf. All he could deduce is that she was a very pretty woman. Henry noticed that Kim always drove by on Tuesdays and Thursdays. She left home at 10am and returned about 3 pm. He wondered where she went but knew it was none of his business. He knew better than to ask her any personal questions because on those rare occasions, he did, Kim always changed the subject. If Kim wanted Henry to know her business, she'd tell him. This he understood.

It was now July and Steven was in the second month of summer vacation from school. As did Ashley decades before, Steven spent most summer days playing at the beach. Kim, always wearing her sunglasses and headscarf, spent a lot of time there with Steven. After walking Steven down the trail to the shoreline, Henry usually stayed and watched from the bluff. He noticed that when he was at the beach with Steven, Kim stayed in her house. Whenever he saw Kim go down to the beach to play with Steven and he would go down to join them, within an hour of his arrival Kim would say she had something that needed her attention at home.

One day while walking on the beach, Kim noticed Steven swimming below the bluff like he did so many times, but today was different. Steven found himself caught in a riptide and was being pulled out to sea. She ran to shore as fast as she could, removed her sunglasses, headscarf, and a black wig, and dove into the water and swam out to rescue Steven.

As she got closer to Steven she noticed he had broken away from the riptide and was now trying to swim back to shore. When she swam up to him and got a hold of him, Steven was exhausted after using all his energy fighting the pull of the riptide. When they reached the shore they were both very tired and just laid on the beach for a few minutes.

After making sure Steven was OK, Kim jumped to her feet, retrieved the wig and placed it back on her head along with her sunglasses and headscarf. Steven had noticed that Kim did not have any hair under the wig and wondered why.

"You better go home and rest, Steven," said Kim. "That's probably enough beach time for you today."

Kim returned home, and so did Steven, who told his grandad what happened, how Kim saved his life. The one time Henry decided he could take his eyes off Steven for a few minutes turned out to be the one time Steven got into trouble. Henry promised himself that he'd never again take his eyes of the boy when he went swimming in the ocean.

He also told Henry that Kim wore a wig and was bald underneath it. Henry drove to Kim's house to thank her for saving Steven's life. Henry knocked on Kim's door but nobody answered so he waited a few moments before knocking again.

Still there was no answer, so he and Steven drove home. A few minutes later he saw Kim drive up and went out to greet her.

"I'm sorry," she said. "I couldn't come to the door when you were at my place. I just wanted to make sure Steven was okay."

Henry thanked Kim for saving Steven and invited her inside. After living next door for nearly a year now, this was the first time she accepted the invitation to come in the house. Once inside, Kim did not take off her sunglasses. Head moving back and forth, up and down, Henry noticed she was extremely interested in how the house looked.

She said, "I just love old homes and so glad you invited me in. Thank you, Henry."

"Of course. Welcome," said Henry. "What do you think of our house?"

"It brings back memories," said Kim.

"Did you grow up in a Victorian home?" Henry asked.

"I love the rose bushes along the fence," said Kim. "Roses are my favorite flower."

"Ashley and I planted several rose bushes together," said Henry. "Did you have rose bushes at your home when you were a little girl?"

"Oh my, look at the time," said Kim glancing down at her watch. "I have a phone call to make. Thanks for inviting me inside Henry. See you soon down at the beach, Steven."

How could Henry now not put two and two together? It could only mean one thing: Kim must have cancer and was going through chemotherapy. Henry had gone through the same thing with his wife and knew the side effects of the treatment. Like Kim, Victoria wore a wig to hide her hair loss, too. Henry never let on that he knew about the wig.

Henry figured Kim must have been going to treatment on Tuesdays and Thursdays since she left and returned at the same exact times. What else could it mean? This must have been the reason Kim moved to the isolated house here in Cambria, to get away from people while she was going through chemo. He wondered silently why Kim never had visitors. Someone must know her, love her, and care that she is sick.

Judging by never seeing anyone drive to Kim's house, Henry and Steven were the only friends Kim had, and they became closer and closer as friends over time. Another year had now passed. Henry figured that her chemo must have stopped because she no longer drove by on Tuesday mornings. She did leave on Thursdays and, like clockwork returned at noon instead of 3pm like she used to do. She was still wearing the wig, which Henry thought was strange. He thought her hair would have grown back by now. She looked like she was doing great.

Kim began leaving her house more and more and often seen eating in Cambria at El Toro, her favorite place as she told Steven. Kim would eat dinner there several days a week and then walk the streets of Cambria, always stopping at the wishing well next to Mr. Higgins' Antiques and throwing in a coin for luck before her drive back to the cottage by the sea.

One Saturday, Henry, and Steven spent the morning at the beach using the metal detector Henry purchased looking for some of that long-hidden pirate gold rumored to be buried under the sand. They noticed Kim in her bathing suit walking their way.

"Hi neighbors," she said. "What-cha' doin'?"

"We're searching for gold buried by pirates!" said Steven.

"Can I join you?" asked Kim.

"Of course you can," said Henry.

As they walked the beach together, Henry noticed a scar on the back of Kim's leg just above her ankle. He wondered how it got there but knew better than to ask. Though he and Kim had become very good friends, Kim still did not share details about her past. Henry remembered how Ashley, when she was 8, had fallen on the trail while walking down to the beach and had cut her leg very badly on the bluff's sharp rocks. The wound left a scar on her leg too. Henry did not think much more about it; his mind was on the sound of the metal detector.

That night all Henry could think about was the scar on Kim's leg. Kim was in her early-'30s at the oldest, so was around the same age as his Ashley would have been had she been alive today. The fact that the scar was in the exact same place as Ashley's bothered him.

Was Ashley alive? Could Kim be Ashley? Was this the reason why she always wore sunglasses and a headscarf? Did she wear the wig to hide her blonde hair? Why would Ashley hide her identity from her own dad and son? After writing the letter Henry found in the mailbox, could Ashley be afraid to come home as Ashley?

The next day, Henry decided to walk to Kim's house, or should he say Ashley's? Now he was sure this was his daughter. He could see the backyard of the cottage, and in the yard was a blonde-headed woman, not wearing sunglasses, putting some clothes on the line to dry. She could not see Henry coming, and Henry really did not want Kim to see him approaching.

As Henry came closer he was able to see her face clearly. Though Henry had not seen Ashley since she was 17, the woman he was now looking at looked a lot like Ashley after putting about a dozen years on her. His heart was pounding. His Ashley was indeed home! He wanted to run over to her, grab her, and give her the biggest hug ever, but he held back.

Henry had to think out how best to manage this. He knew his daughter was trying to hide who she was for some reason and the timing might not be right for her. He had to think of her feelings and honor her wishes for the time being. He slowly backed up, silently turned around, and returned home. He could not let Ashley know that he saw her.

Henry wanted his daughter back home with him and with what he knew about her, he knew sooner or later he had to let her know that he knew who she was. He wanted Steven to know this was his mother. But, he also knew it would be best for Ashley to reveal herself when she felt the time was right for her.

Nighttime fell on the Victorian home with joy in the heart of a man that just found his daughter again. Henry knew he would find himself having a tough time sleeping with all the thoughts racing through his mind. He decided to invite "Kim" to dinner at El Toro. Maybe then she would open up. How could he get any sleep tonight knowing what he knew?

Henry recently changed his Will, leaving everything he owned when he died to Steven. Now that his Ashley was back, and as soon as he was certain that Kim was really Ashley, he would need to visit the attorney in town to amend his Will, leaving half of his estate to Ashley and the other half to Steven when he turned 18.

A few days later, Kim or Ashley, whichever it really was, knocked on Henry's door. She said she just wanted to talk. She still wore her sunglasses and head scarf.

"Hi, Henry. Am I interrupting anything," Kim asked.

"Not at all. Come on in. I always welcome your company," said Henry. "How are you doing today? Can I offer you something cold to drink? How about some sun tea?"

"Sun tea sounds great. Thank you, Henry," Kim answered. "I love sun tea. My mom and I used to make sun tea for my dad when he was working in the yard. My mom, dad, and I would sit on the porch and drink the tea together whenever he took a break."

Henry poured two glasses of sun tea and suggested they sit on the porch together while they enjoyed the refreshment.

"Where's Steven?" Kim asked.

"He's in town helping Carol at the Inn," Henry answered.

"Steven is a fine young man," Kim said.

"Yes, he is. He means everything to me," said Henry.

"There's something I want to share with you, Henry," Ashley began. "I'm sure you've noticed that I seem evasive. It's just that I'm a very private person."

"You're not obligated to explain yourself, Kim," said Henry.

"Thank you, Henry," she replied. "Anyway, this is very personal, but I want you to know that I had breast cancer when I moved here. I'm cured now, thanks be to God."

"That's great news, Kim. My wife, Victoria, died from cancer," said Henry.

"I moved to Cambria to be by myself and deal with my illness alone. That may sound odd, but that's where I was at mentally and emotionally," Kim said as she removed her sunglasses exposing her pretty blue eyes that Henry just knew were under the sunglasses. It was as if she wanted Henry to see and figure out for himself who she really was.

She sat there silently, looking into Henry's eyes as if to say, "Hello, dad. It's Ashley." Henry did not know if he could hold back or not, he wanted to hold her so much. It had been far too many years, and now she was here. Henry wondered why she didn't just say it, say, "I'm Ashley, Dad, and I'm home."

"Wait here for a moment, Kim. I want to share something with you," said Henry, who then walked inside and grabbed a box from the trunk sitting beside the couch. Inside the box were pictures of Ashley, which he showed to Kim, hoping this would coax her into ending her charade.

"These are pictures of my beloved Ashley, Steven's mom," Henry said, handing them to Kim.

"Oh, my word! She's beautiful! I see Steven in her. The resemblance is clear," Kim said. "You must miss her something terrible."

Choking back tears, Henry nodded while Kim looked intently at every picture as if to say, "I remember this picture." But she never made a single comment other than telling Henry over and over that he had a very beautiful daughter.

Henry and Kim spent about 20 minutes thumbing through the photographs and drinking sun tea until Kim said, "Well, Henry. I do need to get going. I have a few things that need my attention at home. I just wanted to come by and tell you about my health. You've been so kind to me and we've grown close. I feel like I owed you the honesty," said Kim. "Thanks for the sun tea. Let Steven know I was here and missed his company."

"Okay, Kim. Any time. Hope to see you again soon," said Henry. "Stop by any time."

Days passed and still the woman had not said a thing about being Ashley. She began visiting Henry every day, bringing sun tea with her for both of them to drink while they waited for Steven to arrive home from school. They sat on the porch swing together, just like Ashley and Henry did so many years ago talking about dad/daughter type things. Each day she came, another piece of the puzzle seemed to fit.

Eventually, Kim began to open up about her past. She told Henry that she left home to be with a man when she was a teenager and moved to Los Angeles before relocating to Ohio, where she lived for several years.

"It was a big mistake. I should have listened to my dad. He knew the guy was a creep and no good," said Kim. "But love is blind. At least, I thought I was in love. I was wrong."

"We all make mistakes, Kim. All of us. The best we can do is acknowledge our errors in judgement, learn from our mistakes, and move forward," Henry said.

"You're very wise, Henry. You remind me a lot of my dad. I miss him," said Kim.

"Where is your dad now, Kim? Is he still alive? If so, maybe you should call or visit him and tell him how you feel," said Henry. "I bet he'd be glad to hear from you after all these years. We dads are very forgiving."

"The sun tea is delicious," said Kim, changing the subject as she always did. "By the way, I wasn't honest with you a few years back when you asked me about being married."

"Oh," said Henry.

"Yes. I'm a widow. Up until now, it's been too painful to talk about. My husband died in a car accident," said Kim. "I don't wear my wedding ring for two reasons: it reminds me of the pain of losing my husband, Bill, and I'm afraid I'll lose it, so I leave it in a drawer at home for safe keeping."

Everything written in the letter Henry found was now coming from the mouth of this woman. Henry did not understand why Ashley did not reveal herself. She had to know that by now Henry had figured it out. Was she waiting for Henry to be the one to say her name? Consumed with shame, was this Ashley's way of rejoining the family?

Chapter 6
What You're Telling Me Can't Be True

On Henry's 63rd birthday, he invited Ashley to the house to enjoy cake and ice cream with him and Steven. Though no longer concealing her identity under a head scarf and behind sunglasses, Ashley still was hiding behind the name Kim Brooks, and Henry was still playing along with her game. He knew who she was and that was all that counted.

Henry's health was failing lately, and even now, on his birthday he really did not feel that good, but he wanted his family together like they used to be on his birthdays so many years ago. Henry had been going to see Dr. Woods who was unable to put his finger on what was causing the trouble. After different tests Henry would be given a new prescription, but none of the medicine seemed to be working.

Henry wasn't getting any better and decided that going to his attorney to amend his Will was his best move, even though Ashley had yet to reveal who she was. He had Ashley drive him to see the lawyer. She waited in the car while Henry took care of his business. Afterwards, on their ride back home, he told Ashley what he had done, knowing that even though she did not say who she was, she knew that Henry had taken care of her.

A few weeks later, Henry found himself bedridden. Ashley was at his side, helping every day. She prepared his meals and always gave him the sun tea he enjoyed drinking with her. The family doctor made a trip to the house and noticed Henry was not improving, so called for an ambulance; Henry had to be placed in the hospital for more testing.

Ashley visited Henry in the hospital every day and brought Steven there after school. Henry was getting worse and worse. Then, finally, a test ordered by Dr. Woods shed light on what may have been making Henry so ill. It appeared that Henry's red blood cells had decreased in production. This could be a sign of his marrow not functioning. Now, Dr. Woods had to uncover why. One disease that could cause the problem is a relatively rare disease called aplastic anemia. Its cause was still unknown to medical science and difficult to treat.

Though fearing his days were numbered, Henry still did not tell Steven that Kim was really Ashley, his mother. He decided it was best for Ashley to reveal herself to her son. He thought when the right time came, she would tell him on her own. Ashley and Steven were growing closer by the day. With Henry in the hospital, Ashley became Steven's full-time caretaker.

More and more tests were run on Henry's blood, and more answers were coming out. It was confirmed that he indeed had aplastic anemia. Dr. Woods found that it was secondary aplasia, a more common strain of the disease, although still rare. Aplastic anemia generally develops slowly, and its symptoms depend on which cells are affected. The cause can be due to radiation exposure or many of the chemo-therapeutic drugs used in cancer treatment. Dr. Woods knew these two options could be ruled out since Henry didn't work around any type of radiation and he didn't undergo any form of chemo.

The next cause could be brought about by drugs or toxic substances Dr. Woods knew Henry was not taking any drugs except what he had given him and they would not cause the problem. The next question then was what toxic substances could Henry have been exposed to? Henry worked in his yard a lot and sprayed pesticide on his flowers and herbicide on the walking trail down to the beach to kill weeds. The problem with this theory was that Henry was not exposed to weed- and bug-killing chemicals while he was in the hospital, so how could his condition be worsening each day?

Dr. Woods knew if he was going to save Henry's life, he had to have a blood transfusion until the marrow began functioning again, followed by antibiotic treatments to fight infection. After that, it was a matter of wait-and-see. If toxic agents were responsible for making Henry sick, this treatment gave him a chance. Otherwise, the prognosis was poor. About half of severe anemia patients succumb to bleeding or infection within a year.

A bone marrow transplant was an option if a compatible donor was available. His daughter presented the best chance of being a good donor match but due to his age – if Henry had been under 40 years old, his chances would be better – and the cancer and chemo she went through, Ashley's donating marrow was not possible.

After the successful transfusion, Henry was not getting any better at all. Dr. Woods ordered a blood spectrum analysis, convinced that whatever was making Henry ill must not be a toxin since the blood transfusion would have cleared the toxins from his body, and Henry was not exposed to toxins after the treatment.

The blood spectrum showed arsenic poisoning. Dr. Woods could not explain how arsenic was getting into Henry's blood. The doctor decided to perform a second blood spectrum analysis in two days and compare these results with the first analysis. The second analysis showed an increase in the level of arsenic in Henry's blood. This could only mean one thing: Henry was now receiving arsenic while in the hospital.

"Are you taking any over-the-counter medications I don't know about, Henry," Dr. Woods asked.

"Nothing, Doc. The only meds I take are the ones prescribed by you," Henry answered.

"Are you eating or drinking something brought in to you from outside the hospital," asked Dr. Woods.

Thinking for a moment, Henry answered, "Yes. Kim brings me sun tea when she visits me every day."

"Is Kim planning to see you today, Henry," asked Dr. Woods.

"Yes. She shows up every day around 10 o'clock, and then again with Steven in the afternoon after school lets out," said Henry.

"Don't drink the sun tea today. After she pours you a glass full, pretend that you're feeling especially weak and need some sleep. Tell her to leave the tea so you can drink it when you wake up," Dr. Woods instructed.

"What are you suggesting, Dr. Woods? That Kim is poisoning me? That's preposterous!" said an indignant Henry.

Henry could not believe what the doctor was telling him. Why would the daughter that he loved so much, and who he believed loved him back, want to kill him? If the sun tea contained arsenic, it had to be getting into the tea without Ashley knowing it, Henry thought. But if that were the case, wouldn't Ashley and Steven also be getting sick?

"I'm not saying Kim is poisoning you, Henry. I'm saying that there may be arsenic in the sun tea that is making you sick," Dr. Woods explained. "I want to have the tea tested."

Ashley came to visit at 10am sharp as she did every day. And, as she did every day, she brought along sun tea.

"Hi Henry. How are you feeling today? Any better?" Kim asked before pouring Henry a glass of sun tea.

"Not too good, Kim, not good at all. I'm feeling very weak," Henry feigned. "I hate to disappoint you but I think I need to get some sleep, and I'll see you later this afternoon when you come back with Steven."

"I'm sorry to hear that," Kim said, giving Henry a kiss on the forehead. "I'll see you this afternoon with Steven and fresh sun tea."

"You can leave the glass of tea you just poured and I'll drink it as soon as I wake up," said Henry. "It'll make me feel better."

Henry did as Dr. Woods instructed, and as soon as Ashley left, Dr. Woods had the sun tea tested. The lab result revealed the sun tea was loaded with arsenic. Henry refused to believe Ashley was poisoning his sun tea but there just no other explanation. But why? Why would she try to kill her father? She had been such a daddy's girl growing up until she left home. Had she begun hating him, blaming Henry for the poor decisions she made? Had she lost all feelings for her father?

Henry insisted that there must be a mistake and told Dr. Woods he wanted a second test on the sun tea Ashley brought with her in the afternoon. Dr. Woods agreed. The second test result was no different than the first. The sun tea, once again, was loaded with arsenic. It was time to call the police and file a report.

Due to the nature of the case – essentially a crime in progress – a detective was immediately assigned to investigate. Detective Robert Barnes interviewed Dr. Woods and Henry that evening, went to the courthouse the next morning, and petitioned a judge to authorize a search warrant to search Ashley's house for arsenic.

Ashley was at home and Steven was there with her when Detective Barnes arrived. He was accompanied by a second detective, three uniformed officers – one of them a female officer to arrest Ashley on an attempted murder charge – and a social worker to place Steven in a temporary home until Henry was released from the hospital.

The search uncovered two suspicious items: two small cans with an unknown powdery substance inside. One was found in the garage, and one under the kitchen sink. A large jar of sun tea placed on the front porch was also taken for testing. If no arsenic was found, Ashley would be released. If arsenic was found, she would remain in custody.

The tests came back conclusive. Both cans and the sun tea had arsenic in them, and Ashley was formally charged with the attempted murder of her father, Henry Benson. Steven was taken to Carol's house to stay with her. Cambria PD requested Ashley's DMV record from Sacramento to cross-check her fingerprints since Ashley obtained a driver's license after she ran away with Bill and lived in Los Angeles before moving to Ohio.

When the fingerprint record arrived at the police department the next afternoon, Ashley's booking fingerprints were compared with her DMV fingerprints and they did not match. A DMV record search under the name Kim Brooks came up empty; there was no Kim Brooks on file anywhere near the age, height, and eye color matching the arrested person's description.

When Detective Barnes went to see Henry in the hospital to share the facts of the case thus far, Henry was in complete shock when he heard the news.

"I don't understand, detective. How could she look so similar to Ashley? She even has a scar on the back of her leg just like Ashley has. There's got to be some mix-up with the DMV fingerprint record," said Henry, sobbing.

"Regardless, Mr. Benson," said Detective Banes. "Whoever this person is, facts are facts, and the facts of the matter show that she was serving you arsenic-laced sun tea, and we found arsenic at her home, too, in two jars."

"What now, Detective Barnes," asked Henry. "And where is Steven?"

"Steven is safe and sound with Carol at the Seaside Inn. Carol said he can stay with her as long as necessary," said Detective Barnes. "As far as the woman claiming to be your daughter, we have an imposter yet to be identified. We've sent her prints to the FBI for further review. We'll update you as soon as we hear something. Rest well, Mr. Benson."

It would be several days before FBI would have an answer. In the meantime, Detective Barnes re-interviewed the woman they had in custody.

"What's your name?" asked Detective Barnes.

"I'm Ashley Benson, Henry Benson's daughter like I've been telling you," said the woman.

"Not true. You're lying. Your fingerprints do not match Ashley Benson's fingerprints," said Detective Benson.

"Then there's obviously a mistake," said the woman.

"Your prints have been sent to Washington D.C. for evaluation by the FBI; we'll know soon enough what your name is," said Detective Benson. "Make things easy on yourself by telling me who you really are. If you don't, an additional charge of providing false statements to an officer will be added to your charges."

"I told you, officer. I'm Ashley Benson," said the woman.

"Fine. Okay. Ashley Benson, why were you spiking sun tea with arsenic and giving it to your father to drink?" asked Detective Barnes.

"I don't know what you're talking about?" said the woman.

"We found arsenic stored in two other locations at your cottage," said Detective Barnes. "Tell me the truth and make things easier on yourself. Confess and the district attorney will ask the judge for leniency in sentencing."

"I don't know what you're talking about when it comes to arsenic. Why on earth would I poison my own dad?" she said.

Detective Barnes knew the woman was sticking to her story and his best option was to end the interview and wait for an answer from FBI. When the fingerprint analysis did come back, FBI identified the woman being held in the Cambria jail as 38-year-old Sarah Miller. Sarah had a lengthy rap sheet that included several felony charges of grand theft, passing bad checks, forgery, and identity theft. Also included were nearly a dozen misdemeanor charges for petty theft, disorderly conduct, vagrancy, and being drunk in public.

Most telling was an All Points Bulletin for Sarah Miller's arrest on charges of murder of one Sam Watson in the first degree. Sam Watson died at 83. He lived alone until he was diagnosed with cancer, which is when Sarah Miller, an in-home-care specialist, was assigned by her company to care for him.

After caring for Sam for one year, Sam changed his Will, naming Sarah Miller as the sole beneficiary of his estate and a $10,000 life insurance settlement. When she received the insurance money, Henry Watson, Sam's only son, suspecting foul play, hired an attorney to challenge the settlement. Sam's body was exhumed, an autopsy performed, and traces of arsenic were found in his hair. Poisoning, not natural causes, became listed as the official cause of death. Sarah and the $10,000 were long gone by this point.

Cambria PD notified the county district attorney in Ohio having jurisdiction that they were holding Sarah on a murder charge and preparing her for extradition. Detective Benson informed Sarah that the jig was up. Sarah was under the belief that if she confessed to the crime of poisoning Henry – attempted murder – she would not return to Ohio to face a more serious murder charge. She was wrong, but Detective Barnes did not disabuse her of the misconception.

Sarah explained that she met and befriended Ashley Benson about five years ago at an alcohol rehab in Ohio. She said Ashley told her all about her life, that her dad and mom, which she had not seen in several years, lived in Cambria and had a fortune. When Sarah checked Ashely's story she discovered that Ashley's mom had died and her dad moved to Mojave. By the time she decided to come to California and pose as Ashley, she found out that Henry had moved back to Cambria.

"What about the scar on the back of your left leg?" asked Detective Benson.

"I noticed Ashley had a scar so I took a piece of glass and cut myself deep enough in the exact same place to leave a similar scar to better fool the old man," Sarah explained.

"Why the silent treatment? Why did you never tell Mr. Benson that you were Ashley?" the detective asked.

"I wanted the old man to start putting it together in his own mind, which would make it more believable," said Sarah.

While Henry continued his recovery in the hospital, Sarah Miller was extradited to Ohio. Detective Benson told Henry if an Ohio jury failed to convict Sarah Miller, she would be extradited back to California to stand trial for his attempted murder.

"Sarah said she was in rehab with Ashley about five years ago. If she's telling the truth, then that means Ashley did not die while giving birth to Steven," Henry said to Detective Benson. "That means she may still be alive! Can Cambria PD help me find her?"

"The best I can do is inquire if Ashley has been arrested anywhere in California. This would give us her whereabouts at the time of arrest," said Detective Benson. "If that comes up empty then your best bet is speaking with a private investigator. I'll let you know what I found out as soon I as I find out."

Henry was released from the hospital about one week later and hired an in-home-care specialist. Steven returned home too. Carol stopped by every morning and evening with food and to keep the house tidy and clean. A few days after being home, Detective Barnes went to see Henry to tell him there is no record of Ashley Barnes being arrested in the state.

Henry called the captain of the police department in the Ohio town where Sarah was being held and asked if he could recommend a top notch PI. The captain gave Henry the contact info for an investigator in Bowling Green named James White.

Chapter 7

If My Daughter Is Alive, Find My Daughter

James White found out that a woman named Ashley Benson had indeed been admitted to an alcohol and drug treatment center in Ohio in 1953, corroborating Sarah Miller's story and timeline. A staff member told James that she remembers Ashley saying she planned on moving to Arizona after being released from the treatment center.

The PI learned that Ashley obtained a driver's license in Arizona that listed an address in Flagstaff shortly after leaving Ohio. He asked a colleague in Flagstaff to visit the address to locate Ashley, which he did, but Ashley no longer lived there. The next-door neighbor told the PI that Ashley mentioned she and her boyfriend, Dennis Swanson, were moving to Los Angeles, California.

James discovered that there were 22 men named Dennis Swanson living in Los Angeles. He obtained their phone numbers from the telephone company and one by one he called them. The second to the last Dennis Swanson was the one he was looking for however, Dennis told James that he and Ashley broke up about a year ago and he had not heard from her since.

Cooperative, Dennis agreed to answer questions to help James find Ashley.

"What did Ashley do for work," James asked.

"Nothing," said Dennis. "I provided and paid all the bills. Ashley was a homemaker and a darn good one at that, if I may say so."

"So why did the two of you break up? Infidelity? Drugs?" asked James.

"None of the above. We grew apart, so to speak," said Dennis.

"It happens," said James.

"Yeah, too bad. I really loved that woman at one time," said Dennis. "Good woman."

"Any idea where she went to or how she planned on putting a roof over her head without an income," asked James.

"No idea," said Dennis.

"Did she have friends that you may think maybe putting her up?" James asked.

"Ashley kept to herself. She was a wallflower. Our friends were mutual friends. If she was staying with one of them, I would have heard something."

"What about skills? Did Ashley have skills to land a job?" James asked.

"I suppose she could be a maid or a caretaker of some sort," said Dennis. "She did mention from to time how rewarding it would be to find work helping homeless people. Ashley has a heart of gold."

"Did Ashley say how or where she wanted to do this," asked James.

"No. She gave no details," answered Dennis.

"How long where you and Ashley together in California," asked James.

"About a year," said Dennis.

"Did you take weekend trips anywhere within the state, or did Ashley speak fondly of any particular town?" James asked.

"As a matter of fact, now that you ask, we spent many weekends each year in San Francisco, and a few more than that in San Diego," Dennis said. "San Francisco is my favorite city. Ashley hated the weather there; she did not like the cold and damp, so we stopped going. That caused problems in our relationship; I thought she was being selfish."

"Tell me about your time together in San Diego," said James.

"I always found San Diego very bland and boring. Ashley would go on and on about how perfect San Diego's climate is year-round. I got tired of hearing about it. Over and over again, she reminded me no matter the time of year, odds are the high temperature was between 72 and 76 degrees, and the overnight low between 64 and 68 degrees," said Dennis. "She'd go on and on about not understanding why so many people were moving to LA instead of San Diego. It drove me nuts."

"Okay Mr. Swanson. Thanks for your time. Any objections if I have more questions and follow up with you then?" asked James.

"Not at all," Dennis answered.

"Okay, thanks for all your help. Good bye for now," said James.

"Wait. Hold on, Mr. White. One more thing," said Dennis.

"Yes," said James.

"Good luck. I hope you find her," said Dennis. "And if you do, if you wouldn't mind telling Ashely no hard feelings on my part, and that I love her even though it didn't work out."

"Will do, Mr. Swanson," said James. "Thanks again. Good day to you, sir."

"Good day," said Dennis before hanging up.

The conversation with Dennis was chock-full-o clues and a huge hint-and-a-half. Ashley hated the cold and damp, preferred temperately warm weather, and loved San Diego. James moved his search there. He began contacting homeless shelters and missions in San Diego County and struck gold with Angel of Mercy Midnight Mission. Sister Shelly Grace told

him that there was a woman working there named Ashley
Benson.

James hopped on a plane to San Diego to meet and interview
Ashley in person. He did not mention the possible break in the
case to Henry. James knew never to count chickens before the
eggs hatch. Instead, James briefed Henry after taking action on
a lead to let him know what he had been up to and that it led to
another dead end.

James first met with Sister Grace, who walked him to the
fellowship hall where Ashley was helping set up tables and
chairs for the next meal.

"Ashley, do you have a minute for me, please?" asked Sister
Grace with James by her side.

"Of course I do. What do you need for me to do?" said Ashley.

"There's someone I'd like for you to meet. This is James White.
He's a private investigator from Ohio. He'd like to ask you a
few questions," said Sister Grace.

"Hello, Ashley. James White PI," said James, extending his
hand.

"Hello, Mr. White. I'm Ashley Benson," said Ashley, shaking
James' hand. "What can I do for you?"

"I'd like to have a word with you in private. Sister Grace has
been kind enough to allow us to sit and talk in her office," said
James. "I'll follow you."

A former FBI agent, James followed Ashley to Sister Grace's office, taking note of her facial expression, body language, and stride for clues into her demeanor. Was she nervous? Did she display any sign that she may have something to hide?

After they both took a seat, James began. "You are Ashley Benson? Yes?"

"Yes, I am, sir," answered Ashley. "What's this all about? Have I done anything wrong? I don't understand."

"Ashley Benson, born and raised in Cambria, California? Daughter of Henry and Victoria Benson. Mother of Steven Mars?" asked James.

"No. Ashley Benson from Minneapolis, Minnesota," said Ashley.

"Ms. Benson, you're dad, Henry, is not well. He hired me to track you down. He forgives you for running away when you were 17 and feels guilty about it. He blames himself for being too hard on you and chasing you away," said James, closely examining Ashley's reaction, looking for raised eyebrows, which may be a sign that she is surprised she had been found and unsure what to say next.

Instead, Ashley's eyebrows dropped and eyes squinted, a sign of confusion. "Sir, I'm afraid there's a misunderstanding. You have the wrong Ashley Benson," said Ashley. "I'm sorry."

"Ma'am, you're not in trouble, and there's nothing to be afraid of. If you don't want to reconnect with your father and son, then just say so and I'll report your wishes back to your dad," James explained. "I'm under a professional and contractual obligation not to leave here until after I can confirm that you, Ashley Benson, are Henry Benson's daughter. I'm not going to force you to go to Cambria to see your dad. I have no authority to do that."

"Well, now, that's good to know, but no matter because I'm not the Ashley Benson that you're looking for," said Ashley.

"Can you prove this to be the case," James asked.

"I'd love nothing more than to prove this to be the case, Mr. White. But how do I prove it?" asked Ashley.

"Fingerprints. The Ashley Benson I'm searching for has fingerprints on file with the DMV. I have a copy of them," said James. "I'll need you to come with me and I'll take you to the local sheriff's station so they can take your fingerprints, and then we'll compare yours with the Ashley Benson I'm looking for. Are you willing to do this?"

"Yes, I am. I have nothing to hide; I'm not wanted by the police and want to prove that I'm not the Ashley Benson you're looking for. And on top of that, I feel for Mr. Benson. I want him to find his daughter. My helping you will help him."

James and Ashley drove to the San Diego County Sheriff's Department and her fingerprints were taken. On the drive there, James shared details of the case, hoping to tug at Ashley's emotions, enticing her to come clean. After comparing Ashley's fingerprints with the prints on file, there was no match. This Ashley Benson was telling the truth. She was not Henry's daughter. After driving Ashley back to the mission, James phoned Henry to update him that once again his lead was a dead end.

Chapter 8

Ashley Is Found

It was now December 1968, and years had passed since the PI had no new leads. By this point, Henry had spent several thousand dollars. Steven was now 17, the same age as Ashley when she disappeared. Christmas was less than one week away. It would be another Christmas Day without Ashley. Henry knew he was growing old and did not have much time left in life.

Looking out the window, Henry saw a red car driving on the dirt road leading to his house. It pulled into his driveway and parked. A nicely dressed woman who looked to be in her '50s stepped out of the car and walked toward Henry's front door. Henry opened the front door before she got to the porch.

"Hello, sir. Merry Christmas to you," she said.

"Merry Christmas," replied Henry. "How can I help you?"

"My name is Betty Young. Is your name Henry Benson?" she asked.

"Yes, it is," said Henry. "Why do you ask?"

"Do you have a daughter named Ashley?" asked Betty.

"Yes, I do. What is this about?" said Henry. "I'm in no mood for games. If I think you're conning me, I'm calling the police."

"Mr. Benson, I have news for you. I've been caring for Ashley for a few years. Ashley isn't well; she's very sick and wants to come home," said Betty. "We drove here from Mississippi. Ashley took a turn for the worse while we were driving through Oxnard and was admitted to the hospital there. She wants to see you."

"I don't believe you! How dare you toy with an old man's emotions! I'm not well. Who put you up to this?" Henry asked.

"Mr. Benson, I'm telling you the truth," said Betty.

"You'd better prove it, and real quick, or else I'm calling the police," said Henry.

Betty gave Henry the hospital's name and phone number so he could call and verify her story. Henry spoke with a doctor and learned Betty was telling the truth.

"Yes, sir, Mr. Benson. Miss Benson claims that she is your daughter. I asked her several questions to glean some background," said Dr. Schwartz. "Ashley says her mom's name is Victoria. She claims she ran away to be with a man named Bill when she was 17 and gave birth in Ohio to a baby boy she named Steven in 1951. Does this sound about right?"

Henry turned white as a ghost and felt as if he was about to pass out. "I need to sit down," he said, handing the phone to Betty.

"This is Betty," she said into the phone. After listening for a few moments, Betty said, "Yes, of course. Right away. If you wouldn't mind telling Ashley, I think that would be helpful."

After another brief pause, Betty said, "Okay Dr. Schwartz. I'll see you then. Thank you. Goodbye," and hung up the phone.

Henry lay on the couch, crying uncontrollably. His wailing caught the attention of Steven, who was upstairs in his bedroom. Steven ran down the stairs and saw his grandfather on the old blue couch, tears flowing, holding the hand of a strange woman.

"Grandpa! Are you okay? What happened," Steven screamed. Looking at Betty, he said angrily, "Who are you? What are you doing here? What did you do to my grandpa?"

"You must be Steven. Hello, Steven. My name is Betty Young. I think it's best your grandfather tell you what's going on," said Betty.

Steven sat down beside Henry, and when Henry regained a semblance of composure he began telling Steven the news.

"St, St, Ste-ven," Henry began, still crying and hearing hyperventilation. "St, St, Ste-ven. I, I, I ha, ha, have new news. We've found your mu, mu, mu…."

"What? My mom? You found my mom!?" Steven asked.

Henry nodded and then again began weeping. He looked at Betty as if to ask her to fill in Steven, which Betty did. Betty offered to drive Henry to Oxnard, a 170-mile ride one way. Henry asked Steven to pack a bag for both of them because they were going to see Ashley and would be gone for a few days. Steven was scared. He did not want to go with Henry and see his mom. Henry understood and agreed to allow Steven to remain in Cambria with Carol at the Seaside Inn.

Henry and Betty got into the car, and off they went. Betty did most all the talking during the three-hour ride. Henry learned that Ashley had been an alcoholic for many years, and the abuse had taken its toll on her liver. Betty told Henry that Ashley regretted running away and wanted to come home for a long time but only mustered the courage once she learned she was very sick.

Ashley's hospital room was on the third floor at St. Luke's Hospital. Before entering, Henry spoke with the doctor overseeing Ashley's care. Dr. Schwartz told Henry that Ashley suffered from cirrhosis of the liver and the disease was in a late stage.

"Ashley is on antibiotics to reduce the ammonia build-up and a diuretic to reduce fluid retention," Dr. Schwartz explained. "We have her on a low protein diet and are loading her up on vitamins and minerals."

Henry asked the question he knew he wouldn't like the answer to. "How long does she have to live?" Henry asked.

"We're doing everything we can. The rest is up to God. Only He knows the answer to your question. I'm sorry. We're doing everything we can," said Dr. Schwartz.

"I'm ready to see her," said Henry. "Betty tells me that Ashley knows I would be coming here."

"Yes, Ashley has been waiting for you," said Dr. Schwartz.

"I'll wait out here in the hallway, Henry, so the two of you can have some privacy," said Betty.

Though only 37, Ashley looked to be in her late-'50s. Alcohol had taken its toll on her body. Her skin was pale, her eyes shut, and her abdomen and legs swollen. Henry walked to her bedside, took a seat, leaned in near Ashley's ear, and gently whispered, "I love you, Ashley."

Ashley slowly opened her eyes and in a low, weak voice said, "Is that you, daddy?"

Henry could not hold back the tears as he kissed her forehead. He wanted to hug her but was afraid it may cause her physical pain, so he held her hand instead. Ashely, too, began crying a river.

"I've missed you, Ashley. I've been searching for you for years," said Henry. "A private investigator has been searching for you for years."

"I'm so sorry, daddy. I wanted to come home so much but just couldn't bring myself home in the condition I've been in for so many years. Now you have to see me like this," cried Ashley. "I heard you have been looking for me so I was trying to clean myself up to return home. But every time I would get close to staying off alcohol, something seemed to come up, and I would start drinking again."

Ashley told Henry she was diagnosed with liver disease after moving from Ohio to Mississippi and that she met Betty at an AA meeting. "I told Betty I had to see my mom and dad before I died, and she was nice enough to bring me here," said Ashley. "Is mom coming? Where's mom?"

"Ashley, Mom died shortly after you left. Cancer," said Henry.

Henry told Ashley that her son has been living with him since he was 7. "I was ashamed of abandoning him, but I knew I could not care for him. I thought he would fare better in foster care and they would find him a loving home, which I see they did," said Ashley.

The doctor came into the room and told Henry that Ashley needed rest and he should come back tomorrow. Henry got a room at the same motel Betty was staying at and called Carol to tell her the news. Betty volunteered to forgo rest and drive the three hours back to Cambria to pick up Steven and then another three hours back to Oxnard.

"That's too much driving. You need rest," said Henry. "Carol said she would drive Steven here to Oxnard first thing tomorrow morning.

Since Steven never knew his mother, it was easier on him to lose something he never had. He did not want to meet her and felt sad that she was dying, but real feelings for her were just not there. It was as if a stranger was dying.

"Steven, I understand you're conflicted about meeting your mom," said Carol. "I understand that you'd rather not go to Oxnard, but I think you should."

"My mother abandoned me. She didn't love me," said Steven. "Why should I care about her wanting to see me now?"

Sighing, Carol said, "It's complicated. Life can be complicated."

"I don't want to see her. I'm not going to Oxnard. I'm staying here," said Steven.

"Fair enough. I respect your feelings. I understand how you feel. I respect that you do not want to see your mom," said Carol. "But what about your granddad? I know you love him."

"Yes, I love Grandpa. And what about him?" asked Steven.

"I think your grandpa needs you right about now. He could use your support," said Carol. "How about this? How about you agree to let me drive you to Oxnard not to see your mom but to be there to support your grandfather? Nobody will force you to see your mom if you do not want to. I promise you that. What do you think about that plan?"

Steven silently considered Carol's idea. He trusted Carol and knew if she said nobody would force him to see his mom, then she would stand by him and his decision. Steven agreed to go to Oxnard to support his grandfather. Both Carol and Steven were silent the entire ride there the next morning.

When they arrived at the motel, Steven and Henry hugged and began crying.

"I'm so glad you decided to be here for me, Steven," Henry said. "Carol tells me that you're not ready to see your mom so that I won't make you. Okay?"

"Okay," Steven answered.

"Let's get some breakfast and talk. Visiting hours don't begin for another hour or so," said Henry.

Henry, Carol, Betty, and Steven went to eat together at a local diner. Listening to the adults talking about his mom's condition made him begin to feel badly for her and piqued his interest. After breakfast, they drove back to the motel to drop off Steven. Carol agreed to stay there with him while Henry and Betty drove to the hospital.

As the car pulled into the motel parking lot, Steven said, "Grandpa, I'd like to go with you to the hospital. I don't want to see my mom. I just want to be there for you. I'll wait in the hallway. Is that okay?"

"That's just fine," Henry answered.

"Good idea, Steven," said Carol. "And I've got a good idea of my own. How about just the two of you go to the hospital together, and Betty and I will wait here at the motel. Is that okay with you, Betty?"

"Perfect," Betty said. "You can take my car, Henry.

On the ride to the hospital from the motel, Steven asked Henry all kinds of questions about his mother. Henry would not answer most of them; he wanted Steven to ask his mom himself. All Henry told Steven was that his mom was here now, and they needed to take care of her.

"We must make what's left of her life the best we can make of it, Steven," said Henry. "And you must use this time you have left with your mother to get to know her the best you can. I'm sorry things went as they did between you and her, but we cannot change the past. I hope you change your mind about not wanting to see her. It would mean the world to her and everything to me. But nobody's going to force you."

After speaking with Dr. Schwartz for a few minutes, it was now 10 am and visiting hours. The doctor had no idea that Steven had no intention of seeing his mom.

Dr. Schwartz walked them to door leading to Ashley's room and said, "Steven, seeing you is the best medicine for your mom. She's been telling the nurses all morning that meeting you is the best thing that ever happened to her in her entire life. Good luck, son," said Dr. Schwartz, before turning and walking away.

Henry placed his hand on Steven's shoulder and said, "The choice is all yours, Steven."

Steven nodded, and he and Henry walked into Ashley's room together. When they entered, Ashley looked over at the boy standing by Henry and, with a warm, motherly smile said,

"You must be Steven. You look so handsome. You take after your father."

Ashley asked Steven to come closer, and when he did, she took his hand. "I'm your mother. I love you, Steven," she said. "I've always loved you. Please forgive me for not being there for you. Will you do that for me, please?"

Steven didn't know what to say, so just nodded; to him, Ashley was a stranger. They had no bond. He always wanted a mother and father just like so many of his classmates had. Where had this woman been all of his life when he needed her? He understood what his grandfather told him about her hard life but he did not feel sorry for her.

Henry began sobbing. Tears flowed down Ashley's face. Uncomfortable and not knowing what to do, Steven took his eyes off his mom and looked across the room.

"It's okay, Steven. You don't need to say a word. Just having you here for me to look at you means the world to me. Today is the happiest day of my life. I love you, Steven. Can I continue holding your hand?" Ashley asked.

Steven nodded and a tear welled up in his eye and streamed down his face. For the first time in his life, Steven felt a mother's love and more tears followed.

"Daddy, he's beautiful," said Ashley. "Thank you for taking good care of him."

Still weeping, Henry nodded. Ashley stared at Steven for several minutes. Nobody in the room said a word. Steven glanced at his mom a few times, quickly looking away after a second or two. This may have been the happiest day of Ashley's life, but for Steven, it was the most difficult day of his.

When Dr. Schwartz came in to check on Ashley, he said, "Oh my! Well, look at you, Miss Benson! You look mighty happy! I see having your family here has lifted your spirit!"

"Today is the happiest day of my life, doctor," said Ashley. "Have you met my son, Steven?'

"Yes, we met this morning in the hallway outside your room," said Dr. Schwartz. "He's a fine young man."

"And handsome, too!" Ashley added.

"I just come in to check on you and see how you're doing, and it looks like you're doing fantastic," said Dr. Schwartz.

"The nurses will be in after me to administer medication and make sure you're comfortable. Anything I can do for you, Miss Benson? Any questions for me?"

"Yes, one question, doctor. When do I get to go home to Cambria to be with my son?"

"Dr. Schwartz laughed and said, "I'll talk about that in detail with your dad later today. Just know that if your blood work comes back satisfactory and once the proper arrangements are made for proper in-home care, you could be discharged in a few days.”

“It’s Christmas in a few days,” Ashley said.

“Yes, it is,” said Dr. Schwartz.

“Going home on Christmas Day will be the best Christmas present I could ever ask for,” said Ashley.

A few minutes after Dr. Schwartz left the room, a few nurses entered.

“Hello, Mr. Benson. Good to see you again today,” asked one of the nurses. “Who’s this strikingly handsome and strong young man with you?”

“That’s my son, Steven,” interjected Ashley.

“My, aren’t we in a good mood today? A far cry from the condition you were in yesterday,” said the nurse.

“That’s because my son is here,” said Ashley. “Today’s the best day of my entire life!”

“We can see that!” said the nurse.

The nurses got to work taking Ashley’s vital signs. They replaced her IV bag with a new one and administered medication before leaving the room. Steven and Henry spent the entire day in Ashley’s room. Steven didn’t utter a word, and that was okay by Ashley. Henry and his daughter did all the talking while Steven listened. On the third day, Christmas Day, Ashley was discharged from the hospital.

Chapter 9

Ashley Comes Home

Carol and Steven returned to Cambria two days before Christmas to make sure the home was all set to receive Ashley. Her old bedroom and the adjacent guest room for a full-time nurse were nicely fixed up. Henry was sleeping in that guest room but moved down the hall to a room beside Steven's.

Ashley's bed was placed so she could look out the window and see the ocean and the sunset. Henry had a stair-lift installed to lower Ashley down to the first floor so she would not need to spend all her time in the bedroom. Henry hoped being home again would bring back good memories of better times. Ashley looked much better than when Henry first saw her. The swelling in her stomach and legs had gone down. Her skin, though still sallow, was not as discolored as when Henry first saw her in Oxnard.

Carol and Steven purchased a Christmas tree and decorated it and the house. They also hung Christmas lights on the outside. Out of her own pocket, Carol had a huge welcome banner made and hung it on the porch. She also arranged for extra food to be made by the cooks at the Inn so they would have a fantastic Christmas dinner. Steven was by her side, helping with every task. Steven did not have a lot to say about the situation. Carol understood and did not press the issue. She recognized the entire situation was a lot of pressure for a 17-year-old young man.

Near sundown on Christmas Eve, everything that needed to be done was done. "How about you and I spend Christmas Eve together at the Inn? There are a few things I need to check on and it will make for a nice break for both of us," Carol told Steven. "We've been here at the house working nonstop for two days now. That okay by you, Steven?"

"Sure. I'll go upstairs and pack a few things, lock up, and then I'll be ready to go," Steven said.

"I have a few phone calls to make while you do that," Carol said.

Carol phoned Henry at the motel in Oxnard to update him and check on his estimated time of arrival tomorrow. "Henry, we're all set here. Steven and I are going to spend the night at the Inn, and then we'll be back up here first thing in the morning," said Carol. "What time is the in-home nurse expected here tomorrow?"

"Her name is Samantha. I gave her your number at the Inn and your house. She's going to call you tomorrow morning and tell you when she expects to arrive at my house," said Henry. "Most likely, it will be mid-afternoon. How's Steven? He hasn't much to say whenever I've spoken to him these last few days."

“Steven is fine. He’s doing as well as can be expected. The entire situation is a lot for a young man to take in,” said Carol. “What time do you expect to be here tomorrow?”

“Doctor Schwartz wants to keep Ashley here to eat lunch and then release her shortly after that, so we should be home just before sundown,” said Henry. “I invited Betty to spend Christmas Day with us. I told her she can stay through New Year’s Day so we can all celebrate New Year’s Eve together.”

“That’s the decent thing to do,” Carol said. “The house is all decorated. So is the tree, lights and all. And there are gifts under the tree for everybody. Now that I know Betty will be here, I’ll call John Taylor at the craft store, have him open up and meet me there tomorrow morning and grab a few things for Betty so she has gifts to open too.”

“I owe you big time, Carol,” said Henry. “Nonsense. You don’t owe me a thing, Henry. That’s what friends are for.”

“You’re the best, Carol,” Henry said. “Okay. I’d better get going. It’s getting late, and I’m tired.”

“One more thing, Henry,” said Carol. “Sundown tomorrow is 4:45 pm. It will be dark by a quarter after 5:00 pm. If it’s not too much trouble, I was thinking maybe you can time it so as not to arrive earlier than 5.30. This way, Ashely can see the house lit up by all the Christmas lights when she gets here. How does that sound?”

"Will do, Carol. You're the best. It's a three-hour ride. I'll make sure the ambulance doesn't leave until 2.30 at the earliest. I'll let them know why," said Henry. "See you tomorrow night."

"See you tomorrow night, Henry," said Carol. "And Henry, Merry Christmas, Henry. Merry Christmas. Give my love to Ashley."

"Merry Christmas, Carol," said Henry.

"One last thing, Henry Benson," said Carol.

"What's that?" Henry asked.

"When you get here tomorrow night, be a grateful receiver. Not a word, not a single word about what you find except 'Thank you.' Agreed?" Carol said.

"You have my word on that," said Henry. "Merry Christmas, Carol. See you tomorrow night."

Carol and Steven met John Taylor at his shop bright and early the next morning. Carol picked out a few puzzles, picture frames, and sundry crocheting items. She learned what Betty liked when they spent time together in Oxnard. When she went to pay John, he refused the money. That's how things worked in the small town of Cambria; people looked out for one another and considered other locals as being family.

"John, I insist. Take the money," said Carol.

"Not a chance, Carol," said John.

"Fine," said Carol. "Have it your way. I'm not going to argue with you. It is Christmas Day, after all. However, I insist you and Mrs. Taylor stay at the Inn for a week on me. No charge. Don't argue."

"Sold," said John. "Merry Christmas, Carol. Merry Christmas, Steven."

"Merry Christmas, Mr. Taylor," said Steven.

Carol and Steven drove to Jameson's Printer next to pick up Ashley's welcome home banner. Craig Jameson was there waiting on him with two of his workers.

"Merry Christmas, Carol. Merry Christmas, Steven," said Craig. "The banner's in the truck. We'll follow you up to the house and hang it for you."

On the ride home, Steven said, "I can't believe how much everyone around here loves one another. So many people are going out of their way to help us. I love the Christmas spirit."

"Though it's Christmas, the kindness being extended has nothing to do with it being Christmas and everything to do with doing the right thing because it's the right thing to do," explained Carol. "They'd do the same if it was the middle of July. It's one of the things that makes Cambria people special. We care for and support one another. Whatever someone needs, no questions asked. Doing right is its own reward. It's better to give than receive, Steven. You know that. Even if your stubborn old grandpa needs reminding of this from time to time."

Steven sat silently, letting the lesson sink in during the ride home. The banner was hung and Craig and his workers said good bye. Before they left, Carol invited them in for a mug of hot chocolate with a nip of whiskey and tried to give them a few bucks as a thanks for their help on Christmas morning when they should have been home with their families.

Craig and his workers refused the money, prompting Carol to insist that they, too accept, an offer for a free week at the Seaside Inn whenever they wanted, which they gratefully accepted.

It was only 9am now. Ashley was not expected home for another eight hours. Carol made a nice breakfast and then suggested she and Steven spend some time along the seashore together until lunch. Walking along the beach together, Carol sensed the inner turmoil Steven was experiencing and felt badly about it. She decided to keep quiet and leave Steven to his thoughts for several minutes.

"Your grandpa repeatedly told me how much he valued his time together with you down here; the two of you having fun looking for seashells and searching for pirate treasure," said Carol. "It made for some of the best memories of his life."

"I know," Steven said. "Me too; I feel the same way."

"He spent a lot of time here with Ashley too," Carol reminded him.

"I know. He would talk about it from time to time. But not much though," Steven said.

"Any idea why that may be?" Carol asked.

"I don't know. Maybe it was painful for him," said Steven.

"Yes. Bittersweet memories," said Carol. "Your grandad loves you more than life itself, Steven. There's nothing he wouldn't do for you. But I'm sure you're aware of that."

Steven had no reply. He only listened. Recognizing Steven being lost in thought, Carol gave him a few minutes to think about what she just said before adding," Today is a big day for your grandpa. He's been waiting years for this day. Not having Ashley in his life was enough to kill him. You're the reason why he got up every day. You, and you alone. Understand?"

"Yes, I understand," Steven said.

"There's one thing that you can do for your grandpa that will make today an even greater day," Carol said.

"I know. Talk to my mom," Steven said.

"No. He doesn't expect that," said Carol. "Nobody wants to force you to do something you're uncomfortable doing."

"What then?" Steven asked.

"Try," said Carol.

"Try?" Steven replied.

"Yes. Try. Try you're very best to find it within your heart to forgive your mom. And then try to find it within yourself to spend time with her," Carol said.

"I don't know what to say to her," said Steven. "She robbed me of having a mom and a dad. Do you know how hard it was for me to have friends at school that all have a mom and dad?" Steven said.

"Steven, I don't know what that must have been like because I'm not in your shoes, but I do understand that it was hard on you," Carol said.

"So should I say to her?" asked Steven.

"For starters, how about calling her 'mom.' And then just sit with her and listen to whatever she has to say. She's dying, Steven. Once she's gone, she's gone."

"I don't know if I can do that," Steven said. "I don't have it in me."

"Fair enough. How about instead of doing it for your mom, you do it for your grandpa?" asked Carol. "What about that idea? Can you do it for grandpa? He loves you, Steven."

Steven did not answer. He just looked at the sea. Carol said nothing more for several minutes. Then she said, "Promise me that you'll think about it. How's that? Deal?"

"Okay. You've got a deal," Steven said.

"Great! Let's look for some seashells and then it's time to get back up to the house. I'm expecting a call from the live-in nurse and don't want to miss it," said Carol.

As they walked along the shore, the tide was receding. This was the best time to discover seashells that had washed up on the shore.

"Carol! Look!" said Steven, pointing down and then picking up the most colorful and beautiful seashell he had ever seen. It was turquois with red and pink stripes.

"Wow!" said Carol. "I've never seen such a beautiful seashell!"

Steven placed it in his pocket and he and Carol walked the trail up the hill and went home. As they approached the front door, the phone began ringing. It was the nurse calling from the Seaside Inn letting them know that she arrived. Carol told Steven they needed to drive into town and pick her up.

"Can I stay here, Carol?" Steven asked.

"Of course. I'll be back in a jiff," Carol said.

"While Carol was gone, Steven grabbed a Christmas card and wrote a note for his mom. It said, "Merry Christmas, mom. I found this seashell on the beach today and want to give it to you as a Christmas present. I hope you like it. Steven." He placed the card on the table standing next to his mom's bed with the seashell on top and then went into his room, shut the door, and cried.

While Carol was in town, an old Jeep pulled into the driveway. Steven looked out of the window and saw a lady that looked familiar get out, walk to the front door, and knocked. It couldn't be, Steven thought to himself.

From the porch, Steven heard his name called. "Steven! Open up!" the voice said. It was Claire from the diner in Mojave. Steven had not seen or heard from Claire since the day he and his grandpa left Mojave ten years ago.

Steven opened the door. "Miss Claire?" Steven said in disbelief.

"Merry Christmas, Steven! It's so good to see you!" Claire said, giving him a hug so tight it nearly knocked the wind out of him.

He and Claire both cried. "You're grandpa called me the day he saw your mom," Claire said. "He didn't tell you?"

"No," said Steven.

"Well, here I am. He doesn't know I'm here. It's a surprise. I know he's bringing your mom home today. What time do you expect them?"

"This evening after sundown, so my mom will come home when the Christmas lights are on," Steven said.

"Good. We have time. Come with me. Let's park the Jeep around back so he doesn't see it so as not to spoil the surprise," said Claire.

Shortly after that, Carol and the nurse, whose name was Samantha, arrived. Steven introduced Carol to Claire, and Carol introduced Steven and Claire to nurse Samantha, and then Carol had Steven unload the nurse's personal items from the car and carry them upstairs to her room.

It was 1pm, and time for lunch, so Carol prepared a hearty meal for everyone. Samantha and Claire insisted on helping. Afterwards, all four walked down to the shoreline to spend an hour walking on the beach. At 3pm, Carol said it was time to drive to the Inn and bring home the Christmas dinner and desert. All four drove there together.

It was now dusk and Steven was feeling very nervous. The phone rang. It was Henry calling to say they were at the Inn. They were running a little early and needed to delay so Ashley would arrive at dark when the Christmas lights would be in full splendor. He told Ashley they would be stopping at the Inn to pick up Carol.

Once dark, Betty and Henry, followed by the ambulance, made the drive up the hill to home. When Ashely was taken out of the ambulance and placed in the wheelchair, she saw the home adorned in red, white, and green Christmas lights along with a huge banner on the porch that read, "WELCOME HOME, ASHLEY! WE LOVE YOU! MERRY CHRISTMAS!

Steven and Carol stood on the porch. Samantha, the nurse, waited inside. Claire hid in the kitchen to surprise Henry after he walked in. When Ashley saw the guardian angels on the front door, she began crying uncontrollably. The inside of the house smelled like Christmas dinner. The table was all set and a nine-foot tall Noble fir Christmas tree sparkled beneath twinkling and blinking white and red lights. Ashley continued crying as she was wheeled inside. Henry's face glowed as he smiled from ear to ear.

"Oh, daddy! It's beautiful! The house is so beautiful! It's more beautiful than I've ever seen it!" cried Ashley.

Carol insisted the ambulance drivers stay for dinner, which they gladly agreed to do after calling their boss to explain why they would be returning late to drop off the ambulance.

"Who's hungry? Let's eat, drink, and be merry!" said Carol. Looking at Steven, she added, "Let's get on with the best Christmas celebration ever! Steven, grab two more chairs from the back room so our friends, the ambulance drivers, have a place to sit."

All in all, there were eight chairs placed around the table. Everybody took a seat – Ashley sat in her wheelchair – when Henry said, "Looks like there's one too many chairs at the table. Steven, go ahead and move one of the chairs away."

"No, no, Steven. Leave the chairs as they are. We want everyone to have a seat," said Carol.

"Carol, there's only seven of us," said Steven.

"Can't you count? I count eight," said Carol.

"No, there are seven of us. Me, you, Steven, Betty, Samantha, Darren, and Jim. That's seven," said Henry.

"You're forgetting someone, Henry," said Carol.

Just then, Claire walked in from the kitchen and said, "Merry Christmas, Henry!"

"It's a Christmas miracle!' shouted Carol.

Henry began sobbing uncontrollably. Once he regained his composure, Carol put the radio on to a station playing Christmas music and dinner was served. Steven sat beside his mom. Everybody had a great time. After dinner, Carol served coffee and pie à la Mode with vanilla ice cream. The pie choices were pumpkin and apple. Next it was time to sit in the living room and open presents.

"How about starting a fire, Steven?" Henry said.

While Steven did that, the two ambulance men thanked the Benson family for their hospitality and excused themselves after saying, "Merry Christmas, everyone. Merry Christmas! Thank you for dinner. Good luck, Ashley."

Ashley, in her weakened state, grew weary soon after everybody opened gifts. She was placed on the stair lift and brought to her room, where the nurse helped her into bed. There was a bell, the kind used at hotel desks, for Ashley to tap on and ring when she needed something. Samantha left the room, shutting the door behind her, leaving Ashley alone to go to sleep.

But, Ashley did not go to sleep right away. After no more than a minute alone, she began banging on the bell repeatedly, crying out, "Daddy! Daddy!"

Fearing the worst, Henry raced up the stairs. He opened the door and saw Ashely crying. "Look, daddy. Look!" Ashley said, pointing to the seashell and Christmas card Steven gave her. "He loves me, daddy. He loves me!"

Henry read the card, looked at the seashell, and began crying too. He kissed Ashley on the forehead and said, "Welcome home, angel. Merry Christmas."

"Good night, daddy. I love you. I'm going to sleep now. Tell Steven I said 'Thank you," and let him know I love his present and love him too."

"I love you, Ashley. Good night," Henry said, as he walked out of the room and shut the door behind him. He stood just outside the door for a moment, listening to Ashley cry before walking downstairs to rejoin in the celebration. Carol was waiting for him at the bottom of the stairs with a very worried look on her face.

"Is everything okay, Henry? Please tell me Ashley is okay," Carol said.

"Things could not be better," Henry said. He walked to Steven and whispered in his ear, "Your mom loves the Christmas gift and asked that I tell you 'Thank you," and let you know she loves you. Thank you, Steven. I love you too."

Carol asked Henry if he had a minute to help her in the kitchen. There, she asked Henry what happened. Henry told her and Carol ran out of the kitchen to Steven and hugged him without saying a word. No words were needed.

Chapter 10
The First Day of the Rest of Ashley's Life

The next morning was like just old times. Henry woke up bright and early just before sunrise, made a cup of hot coffee, and took a seat in the swing hanging on the porch, watching night turn into daytime while Ashley was upstairs sleeping. The only thing missing was Henry's beloved wife, Victoria. Though physically absent, he knew she was beside him, there in spirit.

Once the sun rose, its rays reflecting on the ocean below, Henry went back inside to begin preparing breakfast for Ashley. However, this morning, there was a lot more food to prepare. His home that day included Samantha, the live-in nurse, Claire, his old friend from Mojave; 4Betty, who drove Ashley to California, Carol, and Steven. It would be breakfast for seven.

Henry got to work breaking eggs, placing bacon in a pan, loading an oven pan with hash browns, and counting out pieces of bread so everyone could enjoy toast with butter and jam. He was making quite the racket in the kitchen. The noise woke up Carol, who came downstairs in her robe to see what all the commotion was about.

"Well, well, well. Look at you," Carol said. "Let me help."

"Good morning, Carol," Henry said with a broad smile across his face.

"And a very good morning to you too, Mr. Benson," said Carol. "You look mighty happy this day after Christmas morning."

"Why wouldn't I be?" laughed Henry. "Today is the happiest day of my life."

"Happiest day of your life? I thought yesterday was the happiest day of your life," said Carol.

"It was," said Henry. "Until today; today is better than yesterday, and tomorrow will be even better than today," Henry explained. "And then the day after that better yet. And so on, and so on, and so on."

Carol and Henry cooked breakfast together, Carol remained quiet. She sensed it would be best to allow Henry to bask in his newfound happiness without her interrupting with small talk. The noise of bacon sizzling and its aroma wafting through the air served as an alarm clock. One by one, each person in Henry's house woke up and made their way downstairs, all except Ashley and Samantha, who was tending to Ashley, helping her prepare for the morning.

When all the food was nearly ready to be served, Henry asked Carol to take over so he could go upstairs and tell Ashley "good morning" and kiss her. Henry walked upstairs to Ashley's room, and as he was about to knock on the door, he heard Ashley crying.

"Ashley, honey? Are you Okay? Can I come in?' Henry asked.

Samantha opened the door, and she had tears in her eyes too. "Good morning, Mr. Benson. Please, come in. All is well. Nothing is alarming, per se. These are the tears of joy!" Samantha explained.

Henry walked into Ashley's room and took a seat on the bed beside Ashley. "Oh, daddy!" Ashley cried. "I love you! It's great to be home!"

"Why the tears, sweetheart?" Henry asked. "Why are you crying?"

"Tears of joy, daddy. These are tears of joy. Smelling bacon cooking made me emotional. It reminded me of when I was a little girl, and you cooked me breakfast every morning," said Ashley. "How silly of me. The smell of bacon makes a grown woman cry."

Henry began crying, too. "Grown woman? No. No matter how old, you'll always be my little girl," Henry said. "Ready to eat? Are you hungry? How do you feel?"

"I feel fantastic, and I'm starved!" Ashley said.

"An appetite! That's the best news I could hear from you," said Samantha. "I'll bring your wheelchair to you, wheel you to the stair lift, and get you downstairs."

"I feel strong enough to walk," Ashley said.

"The news just keeps getting better!" said Samantha. "Mr. Benson, if you wouldn't mind taking the wheelchair downstairs, Ashley and I will be down for breakfast in a minute."

Just then, Steven popped his head in and said, "Good morning, mom. Breakfast is ready."

"Good morning, Steven, my beautiful son that I love beyond what words can describe," Ashley replied. "Do you mind helping your mother walk to the stair lift?'

Henry grabbed the wheelchair and took it to the base of the stairs, ready for Ashley to sit in once she got there. He didn't need to question Ashley why, just a moment ago, she said that she was feeling strong and could walk on her own. As a parent himself, he knew exactly what Ashley was up to: she wanted to be close to Steven, and what better way than asking him for help?

After breakfast, Ashley went back upstairs and climbed back into bed to get some rest. Of course, she asked Steven to help her get there. Once in bed, she thanked Samantha for her help that morning and let her know she'd call on her if she needed anything, and then Ashley asked Steven if he would like to spend a few minutes with her before she took a nap to recharge.

"Steven, I'm so sorry about my past, and I hope you can find it in your heart to forgive me," Ashley said. "I'm sure you have a thousand questions in your head that you'd like to ask me, about why I did what I did, about your dad. I want you to know that you can ask me anything that you want to ask me. I'll answer every question you have. Okay?"

"Okay, mom," Steven said.

"How about taking a seat here on my bed beside me," Ashley said, and Steven did. "I feel a little weak, so please don't be mad if I doze off soon."

"It's okay, mom. I don't mind," said Steven.

"Okay. Thank you, Steven. I love you," said Ashley, who then shut her eyes and fell asleep.

Steven took a seat in the chair next to his mom's bed and watched her sleep until Henry entered the room. "Steven," Henry whispered. "Is your mom sleeping?"

Steven nodded, and then Henry said, "Can you come downstairs with me? I'd like to talk with you."

Henry and Steven sat on the porch swing together for about an hour. Henry told Steven over and over how much he appreciated his giving his mom the benefit of the doubt and showing kindness. Carol, Betty, Samantha, and Claire sat together in the living room together, engaging in small talk.

Ashely woke up around noon and rang the bedside bell, signaling the nurse that she was awake. Henry and Carol made lunch for Ashley – tomato soup and a grilled cheese sandwich – and Steven brought the meal to his mom. Ashley asked

Steven to stay with her while she enjoyed the meal, which he did.

Steven still did not ask his mom questions. Instead, he listened to her talk about her childhood growing up in Cambria. He realized that, though she did not raise him, by virtue of being raised by Henry, they shared many similar experiences. This made Steven love his grandfather even more.

Ashley was still exhausted from the long drive from the hospital in Oxnard to home in Cambria and the excitement of Christmas evening. After eating, she told Steven she was feeling groggy and asked him to stay by her side, which he did, until she fell asleep. When Ashley fell asleep, Steven once again took a seat beside Ashley's bed and watched his mom sleep. Henry peeked in again, but said nothing, shut the door, and went back downstairs where he found all the ladies sitting on the couch, laughing and talking.

"Boy, oh boy, do we have news for you, Mr. Benson," Carol said. Carol liked calling Henry "Mr. Benson," once in a while. "Have a seat, and we'll share it with you."

Henry sat down and said, "I don't like the sound of this, or the looks on your faces. I got a hunch something big is up. I can feel it hanging in the air."

"Well now, Mr. Benson. You're not getting any younger, and neither am I for that matter, and there's nothing wrong with accepting the fact that at our age we can use a little help, and accept that help graciously," said Carol. "Which is something that you really need to work on, Mr. Benson – graciously accepting help, that is."

"Oh, boy. Here it comes. Let's have it. Out with it, Carol," Henry said. "I sense that you ladies have been conspiring behind my back."

"In fact, we have, but it's no longer a conspiracy because now it's coming out in the open," said Carol. "Here goes nothing. We all love you, Ashley, and Steven. So, here's what we decided. I need help at the Inn. Betty has experience working in a hotel and Claire working at a diner, which you know all too well."

"I see where this is going," said Henry.

"Good," said Carol. "Betty is going to help me at the Inn. She's going to stay there until she finds a place to stay in town. This will benefit Ashley; she and Betty are very close."

"Uh-huh," said Henry, feigning outward disapproval, but thrilled inside.

"And Claire will also help me at the Inn; she's going to run the kitchen. The only difference is that Claire will occupy a room at the Inn to call home," said Carol. "This arrangement will free up my schedule to be here for you as you need me. What do you think about all that, Mr. Benson?"

Pausing first, Henry then said, "Well, at least I have Steven. No offense, ladies. But between the three of you, Ashley, and Samantha, I'm outnumbered, five to one. Steven will help me keep my sanity in the face of having so many women trying to boss me around."

"Great!" said Carol. "I already spoke to Steven about the changes, and he's happy about them, by the way….."

"That's because he's still young and doesn't know any better," said Henry, tongue-in-cheek. "Now don't you ladies go babying and spoiling my grandson. I still need to make a man out of him."

"If you say so, Mr. Benson," said Carol. "Now, as I was saying before I was interrupted, I spoke with Steven and he is going to accompany Claire back to Mojave first thing tomorrow morning and help her pack up. Then they'll return the next day."

"Anything else, Miss Hanson?" Henry asked.

Carol silently took note of the "Miss" instead of "Mrs." She took that as a sign that Henry liked her in a romantic way. This suited her just fine, because she was growing fond of Henry in that way too lately.

"Yes, there's one last item," said Carol.

"Pray tell, whatever in the world could that ever be?" Henry said.

"Not a word out of you, not a single word, while we ladies do our best around here to help you make a good home for Ashley and Steven," Carol said sternly. "I'll have none of it. Agreed?"

"Agreed," said Henry.

"It's going to be a wonderful rest of your life, Mr. Benson," said Carol.

"Miss Hanson?" said Henry.

"Yes, Mr. Benson," Carol replied.

"Thank you, Carol," Henry said.

"Henry, you're more welcome than you'll ever know," said Carol.

Henry got up and walked outside to sit on the porch swing. Within a few minutes, Carol joined him and sat at his side. The two said nothing to one another. Words were not necessary. Each knew that the other felt the same way as the other did. And this was just fine with Henry. He had a sense that Victoria might have wanted it this way; that Henry would have a special someone in his life to grow old with, and who better than Carol Hanson? Carol could be trusted to look after Henry's best interest, not seeking personal gain.

The 'Magnificent Seven,' as they began to affectionately refer to themselves, enjoyed a special New Year's Eve celebration together at Henry's house. Henry could not be happier. He did not approve of the overbearing nature of the women who took over Steven. He felt they were spoiling him and treating him like a little boy instead of the young man that he was.

Henry decided to let it slide for now. He planned on having a sit down with all the Magnificent Seven women, minus Ashley, and put his foot down on New Year's Day. Steven was set to graduate high school in June, and the Vietnam War was raging. He feared Steven may get drafted, and if he did, he needed to be as much of a man as he could when he entered military service.

The clock struck midnight, and 1968 was now a memory and 1969 had begun. New Year's Day was here. Henry, Steven, and Ashley watched the college football championship on TV together. Top-ranked Ohio State defeated #2 USC in the Rose Bowl by a score of 27-16. They also enjoyed watching the Orange Bowl, where Penn State defeated Kansas, 15-14. The ladies kept the food and drinks coming while Henry, Steven, and Ashley kept company. Henry and Steven were prohibited from lifting a finger all day.

A week had now passed, and Steven was talking to his mother more and more each day. They began to swap stories about growing up in Cambria. Steven told his mom about collecting seashells and winning 1st Prize at the fair, just like she did when she was a little girl, and how he and Grandpa searched the beach for lost pirate treasure.

Ashley enjoyed listening to her son talk and could tell that Steven really loved her dad. Steven did not question his mom about giving him up after birth; he knew she would be okay with the question but did not want to talk to his mom about anything that made him sad. He only wanted to talk about things that made him happy.

Carol stopped by almost daily to see Henry, Ashley, and Steven, often bringing food with her. Still taking diuretics and antibiotics and no longer drinking alcohol, Ashley's doctor informed them that the scarring of the liver had stopped. The hope was that the liver damage wasn't great enough to cause all-out liver failure.

It was a waiting game, keeping on the lookout for signs of hemorrhaging in the stomach or esophagus. There was also a risk of liver cancer developing, and her body could become poisoned by the ammonia build-up and other body-waste, so she had to be watched remarkably close. Ashley wasn't out of the woods by a long shot.

Feeling a little better every passing day, but still quick to fatigue and needing naps, Ashley began sitting at the edge of the bluff, watching the waves pounding against the rocks and Steven collect seashells. The clean ocean air invigorated her, and the breeze blowing through her hair made her feel like a child again.

James Nelson, who owned the town's only gas station, mail-ordered a pair of binoculars and brought them to Ashley so she could see Steven up close when he was down by the seashore. So many people in town stopped by with gifts for Ashley to make her life easier and more enjoyable.

In the evenings, after dinner, Henry, Steven, and Ashley made a habit of sitting and talking about anything and everything under the sun. Eventually, Henry told her that he had hired a private investigator and how all the leads led to a dead end.

Henry even shared the story about Sarah Miller pretending to be Ashley and then poisoning him with arsenic after learning he amended his Will.

"I remember Sarah from an AA group in Ohio," said Ashley. "She and I grew very close; I shared intimate details of my life with her. I'm sorry she did that to you, Dad. It's my fault."

"Nonsense, Ashley. You're not to blame," said Henry. "Sarah Miller got what she deserved. She was found guilty at trial in Ohio and sentenced to 40 years to life."

"I was lost, dad. I felt terrible about myself and was vulnerable to anyone willing to give me some time and talk," said Ashley. "I should have known better."

"It's all in the past now, Ashley. Forget about it, just like we forget about a bad dream."

Ashley began attending AA meetings every Monday evening, and Henry went right along with her. Sometimes Steven and Carol would go too, but it was rare that they did. The Magnificent Seven spent every Sunday together at Henry's house. They enjoyed a huge dinner together in the late afternoon, and when the weather was nice, a lot of time outside playing board games on a picnic table Henry and Steven built.

Ten months had now passed by. Ashley was doing great and able to care for herself, so Samantha, the full-time nurse, was no longer needed and let go. Days kept going by and things just kept getting better. Ashley was able to walk down the stairs on her own now, the hospital bed was removed, and the Benson house was home to a very happy household.

Finally, after Ashley had been home for nearly a year, Steven began asking questions that had been on his mind since his mom returned home. And just as Ashley promised, she did not become upset by any of his questions. Most of Steven's questions were about his dad.

"Mom, what's my dad's name?" Steven asked.

"His name is Terry. Terry Mars. Just like the planet. That makes you a Martian!" laughed Ashley.

Steven didn't find his mom's joke funny. "How come you and dad didn't keep me?" Steven asked. "Did my dad not love me?"

"Steven, your dad never knew I was pregnant," said Ashley. "I never told him?"

"Why not," Steven asked.

"Shortly after I became pregnant with you before I could tell him, I found out that your dad was married. So I left town," said Ashley.

"What did my dad do for a living?" asked Steven.

"Your father was a highly intelligent man. He owned a business. A hardware store," said Ashley. "He was very successful."

"What did he look like?" Steven asked.

"He was tall, just a bit over 6 feet tall. He had jet-black hair and blue eyes," Ashley said. "Very, very handsome. All the ladies liked him."

"How did the two of you meet?" asked Steven.

"I was with a friend at the lake. Her car wouldn't start, and your father, who happened to be driving through the parking lot, saw us with the car hood up," Ashley explained. "He asked if we needed help."

"Did he get the car started for you?" Steven asked.

"Not exactly. The battery was dead, and neither my friend nor I had money to buy a new battery, so your dad called a tow truck for us," said Ashley. "The tow truck took into town to an auto parts store and your dad bought a battery for us and paid the tow truck driver to install it."

"And then what happened," Steven asked. "How did you end up seeing him again?"

"It was getting late in the day. Your dad heard my stomach growl," said Ashley, beginning to laugh. "I was embarrassed by it. Your dad offered to buy us all dinner at a restaurant. I was head over heels, so of course I agreed."

"Then what happened?" Steven asked.

"After dinner, your dad walked us to the car. I told him that I insisted that he give me his number so I could call him to reimburse him for the battery when I got paid," said Ashley.

"But it wasn't your car; it was your friends car," said Steven. "Why did you offer to pay him back?"

"That's what your dad said, too. He wasn't stupid like I said. So I just told him that I said that because I wanted to see him again," said Ashley.

"Did he give you his phone number," asked Steven.

"No, he couldn't, he was married, remember? Instead, he asked for mine, but I didn't have a phone number, so I gave him my girlfriend's number, the girl I went to the lake with," Ashley said.

"Did you pay him back for the battery?" Steven asked.

"No, I didn't have a job, either," laughed Ashley.

"So, what happened next?" Steven asked.

"Your dad called me at my friend's house several times, and each time, my friend lied, telling him I was at work or just left to go to the grocery store," said Ashley. "My friend always asked your dad for his number so I could call him back, but he never gave one. He would tell my friend that he was calling from work, which he was, and could not accept incoming personal calls."

"Your friend did not ask him for his home number?" Steven asked.

"She did once, but your dad said he was staying with friends, and one of the rules was there was no incoming personal calls unless it was work or family," said Ashley. "I should have known something was up, but I didn't care. I just wanted to see your dad."

"How did he finally get ahold of you?" Steven asked.

"My girlfriend told him to call at a specific time, which he did. I made sure I was there to take the call," said Ashley.

"How long did you and my dad date?" Steven asked.

"About one month. Then I found out that I was pregnant," Ashley said.

Steven began doing the math in his head. A sad look came over his face. He didn't like learning that his mother was like that.

"Steven?" said Ashley. "I know what you're thinking. I wasn't like that with anyone except your father. I promise."

"Okay," Steven said, looking down.

"Steven. I have no regrets. I had you and gave you life," Ashley said. "Just think how much joy you've brought to your grandfather's life."

Steven nodded his head. He understood what his mom meant. "How did you find out my dad was married?" asked Steven.

"I knew something was wrong. Your dad was elusive about his life's details, so after he dropped me off at my friend's house after a date, my friend followed him and found out where he lived," Ashley explained. "I found out I was pregnant with you a few days after that. Then, one morning, we waited down the street from his house, and when he left home, we followed him to find out where he worked."

"Then what happened?" Steven asked.

"My girlfriend went to high school with someone that was a mailman. We gave him the address, and he located the mailman that had your dad's home on his route," said Ashley. "That's how I found out that your dad was married."

"So you left town?" Steven asked.

"Yes, I moved a few towns over. I was crushed. But there was no way I wasn't going to give birth to you," Ashley said. "I promised that I'd take care of myself while I was carrying you, and then give you up for adoption so you'd have a great chance at having a good life; a better life than I could ever give you as a single mom."

"I love you, mom," Steven said.

"I love you, too," Steven.

"I want to find my dad," Steven said. "Will you help me?"

"Of course I will, Steven. Of course I will," said Ashley. "If that's what you want."

Steven finally had a mother, and out there somewhere, a father too.

As Steven and his mom grew closer, so were Carol and Henry; they had become more than just friends. Henry was taking Carol out on dates, and they were very happy together. Carol and Ashley were beginning to grow awfully close too. Carol was a lot like her mother in a lot of ways, and she thought it was great that her dad and Carol were spending time together. Everybody needs somebody to love and love them back.

One afternoon, while Carol and Henry were taking a stroll on the beach, Ashley became extremely ill. She was very confused and began vomiting blood. Steven began panicking. He ran outside and sprinted to the top of the trail.

"Grandpa! Grandpa! Carol! Carol!" he yelled down as loud as he could. "Come quick! Help! I need help!"

Carol and Henry walked up the trail as fast as they could for people their age. In the house and up the stairs they went, out of breath when they arrived at Ashley's room. They saw Ashley lying on the floor with a small pool of blood beside her mouth. Carol ran downstairs and called an ambulance and Ashley's doctor, who arrived at the emergency room a few minutes after the ambulance arrived. Henry, Steven, and Carol drove to the hospital in Henry's old '49 Plymouth. Ashley was admitted into the hospital, and slipped into a coma.

"I'm sorry Mr. Benson," Dr. Turner said to Henry. "Bad news. Ashley is in a coma. Her liver is failing."

"How long, Dr. Turner? How long does she have?" Henry asked, crying, Carol by his side, holding his hand.

"It could be hours. It could be days," Dr. Turner said.

"Can Steven and I sit with her, doctor," asked Henry.

"Of course," Dr. Turner replied.

Henry and Steven did not say a word to one another while they sat by Ashley's bed. Suddenly, Ashley sat up, looked at Steven, smiled, and then fell back onto the bed as quickly as she had risen. Eyes closed, she inhaled deeply, and then exhaled. Ashley had taken her last breath and went into a deep sleep.

Henry broke down in uncontrollable crying while Steven placed his arms around him. Then Henry woke up. He was soaked in sweat. He had just experienced the worst nightmare in his entire life. The year is still 1958, and the time 3am. He and Steven had been at the house in Cambria about one week.

There was no Sarah Miller pretending to be Ashley, no Betty bringing Ashley back home, or nurse Samantha, caring for Ashley once there. Carol was real, as was James White, the private investigator Henry hired shortly after finding Ashley's letter that fell out of the mailbox a few days after moving back into the house with Steven.

Chapter 11

Back to Square One

Henry got out of bed, removed the sheets that were soaked by his sweat, and jumped in the shower. After getting dressed, he went downstairs to the kitchen and made a cup of coffee. The noise of the shower running woke up Steven, who stayed in bed until Henry went downstairs. Then Steven got up and also went downstairs to find out what was the matter; it was unusual for his granddad to take a shower at 3am.

Though only 7 years old, Steven noticed his granddad looked to be in distress.

"Good morning, Grandpa. Are you okay," asked a concerned Steven.

"Steven, what are you doing out of bed at this hour?" Henry asked.

"I heard the shower water and woke up. Are you okay, grandpa?" Steven again asked.

"Fine, fine, I'm fine Steven. There's nothing to worry about," Henry said. "How about going to back to bed? It's too early for you to be up."

"What's the matter, grandpa?" asked Steven.

Henry knew he wasn't fooling Steven with the "everything's okay" spiel and wanted to sooth Steven's concern. "I had a bad dream, that's all," Henry explained. "We all have bad dreams from time to time."

"What was the dream about?" Steven asked. "About me?"

"You were in my dream, yes. And so were your mom, and Carol, and Claire too. And people that do not exist," Henry said.

"Did something bad happen to me in your dream, grandpa?" asked Steven.

"Steven, it was just a dream. Now go back to bed," Henry said.

"I don't think I'm able to go back to sleep," said Steven. "Can I stay up down here with you, grandpa?"

"It's best that you don't. I need some time to clear my mind and gather my thoughts," said Henry. "How about going up to your room and maybe reading a comic book for me. Will you do that for me, Steven?"

"Okay, grandpa," Steven said. "I love you, grandpa."

"I love you too, Steven," Henry replied.

Steven hugged his grandpa, and before turning to walk upstairs to his room, said, "Everything is going to be alright, grandpa. It was just a bad dream. We all have bad dreams from time to time, just like you always say."

Steven went back to his room, and Henry began pacing back and forth across the downstairs. Realizing the noise from his footsteps may keep Steven awake, he decided to take his coffee outside and drink it on the porch swing.

Henry's mind was racing. There were aspects of his dream that gnawed at his soul. He felt that his dream was more like a premonition. Henry was not a religious man; he attended church every Sunday to make Victoria happy. Church was important to Victoria, so it was important to him. Victoria was a very spiritual person. She believed God talks to us in our dreams as well as when we are awake, something Henry dismissed but kept his mouth shut about it out of love and respect for Victoria. Henry believed in reason, chalking off spirituality as nothing more than superstition.

Henry took a seat on the porch swing and began thinking deeply about Victoria's belief that God speaks to us in our dreams. Then Henry began speaking to Victoria in a whisper.

He said, "Victoria, I love you and miss you. I had a bad dream last night, Victoria. I can't shake the feeling that it was more than a dream. Maybe you were right all along about God, and about God speaking to us in dreams. I know that you're dead, Victoria, but at this moment, I feel like you're here with me right now, sitting beside me, wanting to tell me something. Give me a sign, Victoria. Do something so I know you're here with me, listening."

Expecting some sort of sign from the other side, Henry sat still in silence for a few minutes. Before getting up to go inside the house, he said to himself, "Henry, you're losing your mind. Get it together. Victoria is dead, and that's that. There is no other side. There is no God. It's all superstitious hogwash."

Henry walked into the kitchen and made a second cup of coffee. He took a seat on the couch he bought for Victoria and said to himself, "Get a grip, Henry. Snap out of it." Just then, he heard what sounded like the porch swing swinging back and forth. The spindles needed lubrication and squeaked when the swing swung to and fro,

"Must be getting windy outside," Henry said aloud to himself. He walked to a window to take a look and in the moonlight noticed no leaves on the trees were moving. The air was still. There wasn't the slightest of breeze. Curious, he went out on the porch to see what could be causing the noise.

He noticed the porch swing was moving as if someone were sitting on it – it had a symmetrical rhythm, going back and forth at the same slow speed. The chains the swing was suspended from were taut, as if supporting weight.

A chill went down Henry's spine. Goosebumps emerged and the hair on his arms stood straight up. He felt Victoria's presence. Henry walked to the swing, stopped it from swinging, took a step back, and watched as the swing began moving back and forth as before. He thought he heard Victoria's voice beckon him to come and sit beside her, which Henry did.

Henry sat on the swing, stopping its motion. He lifted his feet off the floor without pushing back so the swing would not begin swinging. He sat in the motionless swing for a moment, and then, as if on its own, the swing began swinging back and forth, in the same gentle tempo Victoria liked best when she and Henry sat together looking at the ocean below, not saying a word.

Crying, Henry whispered, "Victoria, help me. Help me. I know you're here, Victoria. What is it you're trying to tell me? What is it that I need to do?"

If what happened next did not happen to him, Henry knew he wouldn't believe the story no matter who told him. Henry, in his head, not audible through his ears, heard Victoria speaking to him, telling Henry, "She's alive, Henry. Ashley is alive."

Then the porch swing stopped swinging, and the feeling that Victoria was there in spirit went away. Henry stood up to go back inside the house. Before he walked through the doorway, he began doubting what just happened. He whispered to himself, "Henry, you're either traumatized by the nightmare, or you're losing your mind. What just happened is nothing more than a hallucination."

As he walked to the doorway, a strong gust of wind began blowing across the porch, and the door slammed shut, leaving Henry face-to-face with the guardian angels carved into the front door. He turned around toward the front yard, saw the trees bending and leaves blowing in the strong wind, and noticed that the porch swing sat completely still.

When he whispered, "Okay, Victoria. I got the message," the wind stopped. Henry opened the door and walked into the house. Before shutting the front door, he took one last look at the porch swing, which, once again, began gently swinging in the still air.

When Henry took a seat at the kitchen table, he heard a loud thump on the porch. It was the daily newspaper. A few days after arriving in Cambria, he ordered a home delivery subscription. He enjoyed reading the news but normally picked a copy in town. He decided to have the paper delivered as a way to get Steven interested in learning about current events.

Henry turned on the porchlight and went outside to bring the newspaper in but first took a glance at the front page. This day was July 29, 1958, the first day of NASA's existence. On the front page, below the fold, he saw a headline that read: "To The Moon, Mars, And Beyond." The subhead read: "Newly Formed Space Agency Promises Exciting New Era Of Space Exploration."

Henry felt something odd inside of him when he read the word "Mars." He reread the headline, saying the planet's name aloud. "Mars. That was Steven's last name in my nightmare. Mars. Couldn't be." As he was about to turn and walk back inside the house, the porch swing moved back and forth a few times, and he once again felt Victoria's presence. Before shutting the front door, Henry stared at the guardian angels carved into the wood, bowed his head, and, for the first time in his life, sincerely prayed to a God that he now believed exists.

When Henry walked into the house, he noticed Steven coming down the stairs. "I thought you were going to go back to sleep, Steven," Henry said.

“I did fall asleep, but I was woken up by what sounded like wind hitting the side of the house,” Steven said. “When I got up and looked out the window, there was no wind.”

“Well, you’re up now. Might as well stay awake. It’s almost sunrise,” Henry said. “I’ll start breakfast. Have a seat here at the table. Here’s the morning newspaper. You can thumb through and find the comics section.”

Before looking for the funnies page, Steven stared at the front page. The NASA story caught his attention. “Grandpa! Did you see this? There’s going to be people on Mars one day!” Steven exclaimed. “I want to go to Mars!”

Steven’s comments made Henry freeze where he stood. Just like the day he and Steven first arrived at the house and his right leg froze when trying to step out of the car, once again, Henry found himself overwhelmed by events. Then a strong gust of wind blew against the side of the house.

Henry and Steven ate breakfast, cleaned up, and went outside to begin work in the yard. Henry was waiting for 8am when James White’s office, the PI he hired, opened. Steven was excited about NASA, and talked all morning about how he wants to be what the newspaper called an “astronaut,” so he could one day live on Mars.

At 8am sharp, Henry called James White’s office. A secretary answered and offered to take a message, explaining that James was unavailable. James called Henry back just after 11am. Waiting for James’ call were the longest three hours of Henry’s life.

"Mr. Benson, James White here. My apology for taking so long to call you back, it's been one hell of a morning," said James.

"I understand," said Henry. "Mr. White, are you a religious man?'

"If you're asking me if I believe in God, then the answer is a resounding yes, though I don't know if I'm what some call 'religious.' Why do you ask, sir?"

"Mr. White, I had an experience last night and this morning," Henry began. "It's something my wife would have classified as a religious experience. If it didn't happen to me, I wouldn't believe it if it happened to someone else and they told me about it. I would have listened politely, smiled, nodded, and considered them crazy. Have you experienced something along these lines; if it hadn't happened to you, you wouldn't believe it."

"Mr. Benson, let me just say this. What some classify as a hunch, others are convinced is a word from God. In my line of work, I've cracked many cases wide open by listening to that voice in my head that wasn't mine," said James. "Does that make sense?"

"I think so, Mr. White," answered Henry.

"Are you a believer, Mr. Benson?" James asked.

"I wasn't until this morning," Henry replied.

“Now, Mr. Benson, as you well know, my services are expensive, so there is no need to justify whatever it is that you want to tell me. Just tell me, and we’ll go from there, sir.”

“Fair enough. I would like for you to do a search in Ohio for Ashley under the last name Mars. Ashley Mars. I have a hunch, or should I say, I believe God spoke to me. I believe searching for Ashley Mars may prove fruitful.”

“Will do, Mr. Benson. I’ll do that as soon as we finish this phone call,” James said. “By the way, Mr. Benson, it’s odd that you mention this.”

“How so, Mr. White?” said Henry.

“I was reading this morning’s newspaper over breakfast with my wife, who happens to have the same name as your beloved wife, Victoria, may she rest in peace, and I was captivated by this new agency called NASA,” said James. “The article mentioned this NASA plans on sending a man to the moon, and then on to Mars. I was reviewing your file when my wife brought the article to my attention; she knows I’ve been infatuated with this NASA program since President Eisenhower said he would be asking Congress to create and fund such an agency.”

“As my wife, Victoria, used to say, “God works in mysterious ways,” Henry said.

“Indeed, Mr. Benson, indeed He does,” replied James. “If that’s all you have for me, I’d like to get started on that search for you. I have a good feeling about this one.”

"Okay, Mr. White, I look forward to hearing back soon with good news," Henry said.

"Talk soon, Mr. Benson. I'm going to say a prayer for you before I begin my search," said James. "Perhaps you can say a prayer for me as well."

"Will do," said Henry, adding, "If Victoria could only hear me now."

"Who's to say she doesn't. Good-bye, Mr. Benson," James said.

Henry hung up the phone, walked outside, sat on the porch swing, and for the second time in his life, sincerely spoke to God. Steven kept working in the garden, weeding around the rose bushes while Henry was spoking to the investigator. When Steven saw his granddad sit on the swing, he took a break and joined him.

"You look different, grandpa. You look happy," Steven said.

"I feel good inside, Steven," Henry said. "I'm ready for lunch. How about we get cleaned up and drive into town to visit Carol and have lunch at the Inn?"

After lunch, Henry took Steven to the ice cream shop and bought him a double strawberry cone. He invited Carol to come along. With ice cream in hand, the threesome walked a few blocks to the park so Steven could play. While Steven was playing, Henry told Carol about his dream and everything else that happened earlier that morning.

“I have a good feeling about this, Henry,” Carol said. “Let’s not stay here too long. I have a hunch you should be home, near your phone.”

Henry and Steven arrived back home at 2.30pm. As they walked up the steps to the front porch, Steven said, “Grandpa, I really like the guardian angels on the front door. I feel like they keep me safe, too.”

As soon as they stepped foot inside, the phone began ringing. It was the private investigator’s office.

“Mr. Benson, This is Shirley Mills, Mr. White’s secretary. Please hold while I patch you through to Mr. White,” said Shirley.

“Mr. Benson, James White here. I’m glad you’re home. Shirley’s been calling you every five minutes for about an hour. I need you to take a seat, Mr. Benson. I have news,” said James.

“I’m sitting,” Henry said. “Don’t sugarcoat anything Mr. White, and no need to preface your remarks. If you have bad news, just give it to me straight.”

“Through the Department of Motor Vehicle records, I discovered that there are 14 people living in Ohio with a driver’s license named Ashley Mars. We got the phone number for each address from the phone company, and Shirley and I began calling each one,” said James. I spoke with a man named Terry Mars living in Akron. I explained the circumstances behind my call, and he handed the phone to his wife. Mr. Benson, we’ve found your daughter.”

Henry began crying.

"Ashley called you right after we spoke. She called me back and told me nobody answered," said James. "Ashley told me she had a doctor's appointment and she will call you again as soon as she returns home, which will be in about an hour. Congratulations, Mr. Benson. Case closed."

"Thank you, Mr. White," Henry said through tears. "Money well spent."

"Mr. Benson, todays services are on the house. No charge," said James. "I hope everything works out between You, Ashley, and Steven."

Henry hung up the phone and began weeping loudly. "What is it, Grandpa?" Steven asked.

"Steven, we've found your mom!" said Henry.

Chapter 12

Going To Ohio

Henry called Carol to tell her the good news. Carol left the Inn and drove to Henry's house to keep him company until Ashley called; though only an hour, she knew it would be an agonizingly long wait. The hour passed, and the phone rang. It was Ashley calling home.

"Hello, daddy. It's Ashley," she said.

Hearing Ashley's voice was like hearing a ghost speak. Was Henry dreaming again, or was it really Ashley? Speechless, Henry began crying again. It took all his effort to talk.

"Ashley, I love you! I miss you and want to see you," Henry said.

"I love you and want to see you too, Daddy," Ashley said, also crying.

"I'm willing to fly to Ohio. I'll take the first flight I can," said Henry. "Is that okay?"

"Yes, daddy. I can't wait. I'll pick you and mom up at the airport," she said.

"Ashley, honey, your mom passed away nearly 10 years ago," said Henry.

"No, Daddy. I want to tell her that I'm sorry I left. I know that I hurt you and Mom," Ashley cried. "Now it's too late."

"Ashley, I'm sure your mom is with you in spirit. Talk to her and tell her. She's listening," said Henry. After a long pause without Henry or Ashley saying a word, Henry said, "I'll have a big surprise for you when I see you."

The next morning, at 5 am, Carol pulled into Henry's driveway. She volunteered to drive them to Los Angeles for the flight to Akron, Ohio. When Henry told her they could fly to Los Angeles from San Luis Obispo, Carol insisted he let her drive them to Los Angeles so they would need to board only one plane.

At 10am, American Airlines Flight 308 left the tarmac and was in the air. Henry and Carol talked with Steven about his grandpa's not telling his mom about him and instead making it a surprise when they landed in Akron. There was no telling how Ashley would react if she heard the news over the phone.

Henry and Steven talked about Steven finally meeting his mother and possibly, his father too. They'd have to wait and find out if Terry Mars was Steven's dad.

"How do you feel, Steven," Henry asked.

"I have butterflies in my stomach," Steven said. "I finally get to meet my mom. I hope she likes me. Do you think she will like me, Grandpa?"

Henry began laughing at the silliness of that question but understood why a 7-year-old in Steven's position would ask it. "Do I think your mom is going to like you? No, Steven, she's not going to like you," Henry said, and then paused for effect before saying, "I think your mom is going to love you!"

This brought a wide smile to Steven's face. "How much longer until we land, Grandpa?" asked Steven.

Henry looked at his watch and told Steven they were scheduled to arrive in less than 30 minutes. They did not talk for the rest of the flight. Instead, they were both lost in their thoughts as they looked out the window.

The airport was now in sight, the landing gear down and locked, and the runway was straight ahead. The plane tipped a little to the left and then to the right as it lined up to the runway for landing. It was only a matter of minutes until Henry would have what he had been waiting on for years.

The plane landed, and the passengers applauded. The captain addressed the passengers over the intercom, saying, "Ladies and gentlemen, welcome to Akron, Ohio. The local time is 5 pm Eastern, and the temperature is 85 degrees. I ask that you remain belted and seated until the plane comes to a full stop at the terminal. On behalf of the crew and stewardesses, I thank you for flying American Airlines."

Henry's heart began racing as the plane pulled into the terminal and came to a stop. "Let's let everyone else exit the plane first, Steven," Henry said. "I need a moment to gather my thoughts. I'm very nervous."

Henry looked behind him and noticed all the passengers were now in front of him. It was time to the exit the plane. Henry unbuckled, stood up, and removed a carry-on bag from the overhead storage bin. Steven unbuckled his seat belt, stood up, took his grandfather's hand, and the two fell in line behind the other passengers exiting the plane.

Ashley stood at the terminal, head and eyes scanning the passengers as they departed. One after another out the plane they came, none of them looking like her father. She began to worry. Maybe my dad changed his mind. Maybe he doesn't want to see me.

Finally, the last two passengers exited the plane. "Daddy!" Ashley screamed, tears running down her cheeks as she sprinted to her father, hugging him. "Daddy, I love you, daddy!"

It had been ten years since Ashley left home in 1948. Now 27 years old, his teenage girl was a young woman. Henry had aged dramatically after going through the stress of Ashley leaving and Victoria dying, and the hot Mojave Desert sun and dry air took its toll on his skin.

Steven just stood there and watched. Then Henry turned to Steven and said, "Ashley, this is your son, Steven. He came to live with me last year."

Ashley couldn't believe her eyes. Steven stared at his mom as she looked at him, smiling and crying. Ashley fell to her knees and was face to face with her son.

"Oh my God! Steven! It's you!" said Ashley. "Can I give you a big hug?"

Steven nodded. Ashley hugged him so tightly that Steven felt the air being squeezed out of his lungs. Ashley rocked him back and forth, sobbing uncontrollably. She then stood up, looked at Henry, and with her hand on Steven's head, said, "This must be my surprise."

Henry nodded. "Why didn't you tell me on the phone that Steven was with you?" she asked.

"I wasn't sure how you would react," said Henry. "Where's your husband, Terry?"

"Steven's father is at home. He wants to give us space. He thought it would be better for us to have this time to ourselves," said Ashley. Looking at Steven, Ashley said, "Are you ready to meet your dad, Steven?"

Steven nodded. Henry picked up his carry-on bag and the threesome walked to baggage claim to grab their suitcases. Henry had his arm around Ashley's shoulder while they walked, and Ashley held Steven's hand. Once Henry grabbed the suitcases, Ashley carried the carry-on, and they walked to Ashley's car, a beat-up 1951 Chevrolet Deluxe.

Ashley lived about four miles from the airport, so it was a short, quick drive. Ashley kept looking at Steven sitting in the backseat through the rearview mirror while she drove.

"I'm so glad you're both here," said Ashley. "Daddy, so many times I wanted to call home, but the time just never felt right. I was afraid that you were so mad at me that you would hang up when you heard my voice."

"Don't be silly, Ashley. I love you," said Henry.

On the ride home, Ashley told Henry and Steven all about Steven's dad – he worked as a clerk at an auto parts store – the house they lived in, and the neighborhood. They lived in a small house in an old part of town on a street with mature trees whose branches formed a canopy over the street and sidewalk.

From the condition of the car and the size of the house, Henry knew that Terry and Ashley were not doing well financially. Henry hated seeing his daughter living in such a poor-looking neighborhood when he had a lot of money.

"Are you and Terry happy together?" Henry asked.

"Yes. Terry treats me like gold. I love him very much, and he loves me," Ashley answered.

Ashley honked the horn as she parked the car into the driveway. Terry came out to meet them. He, like Ashley, was surprised when he saw a 7-year-old-boy with Henry. Terry assumed it was Henry's grandson, but it never crossed his mind that Steven was his son from Ashley.

Terry was the first man Ashley had been with since her husband died in the car wreck; Terry was the married man she wrote about in her letter home. She learned Terry was married and ended the relationship shortly before learning she was with child. Humiliated and feeling used, Ashley skipped town for the duration of her pregnancy, never contacting Terry to tell him about his being a father to the child she was carrying.

Ashley prearranged for baby Steven to be taken and placed into foster care as soon as he was born. She refused to divulge the father's name to the authorities because she did not want to cause Terry trouble. Though she was not happy about his deceiving her, Ashley still loved Terry. She had Steven's last name listed as Benson.

A few months after Steven was born, Ashley moved back to Akron and showed up at Terry's job. This was when she learned Terry was divorced. Love makes us do crazy things. Love makes us forgive and forget, and that is precisely what Ashley did: forgive and forget Terry for his two-timing.

When Terry asked Ashley why she disappeared for a year, Ashley lied and told Terry it was only because she needed time away to get over him, but that time away did not make her forget about him and instead made her realize how deeply she loved him, which is why she returned to Akron.

"Good thing you're divorced now," Ashley told Terry. "Had you not gotten divorced, I had a plan to introduce myself to your wife and tell her everything."

"Why on earth would you do such a thing?" Terry asked. "That would have caused a lot of trouble for me at home."

"Exactly," Ashley said. "Enough trouble, hopefully, that your wife would have kicked you out of the house or walked out on you."

"And then you'd swoop in and have me for yourself," said Terry. "That was your plan?"

"Exactly," said Ashley.

"What makes you so sure that I would have forgiven and forgotten about you being a homewrecker and agree to be with you?" Terry asked.

"I'm not the homewrecker. I had no idea you were married when we met and started dating over a year ago," said Ashley. "You made the choice to have a girlfriend behind your wife's back. Telling your wife about our affair would be your fault."

Terry knew Ashley had a point and had nothing to say in reply. Then Ashley continued, "Do you love me, Terry?"

"Yes," said Terry. "You know I do."

"Do you love me more than you loved your wife?" Ashley asked.

"Yes," Terry answered.

"What were you thinking when I disappeared?" Ashley asked.

"I figured that you somehow found out I was married," Terry said. "And you were hurt, so you left town."

"Why did you divorce your wife while I was away?" Ashely asked.

So, I could be free to find you, and ask you to marry me," Terry said. "I hired a private investigator, but he was unable to locate you. He must not have been very good at his job."

"Or I was good at hiding out," Ashley said. And she was. While pregnant and making arrangements to have Steven placed in foster care, she gave a fake first name and refused to divulge her last name until after Steven was born. This made it impossible for her to be found.

And that was that. Terry and Ashley married within one week of her returning to Akron. Now, seven years later, Terry was about to have his world rocked.

"Daddy, this is my husband, Terry," said Ashley.

"Pleased to meet you, sir," said Terry, extending his hand. "And who do we have here?" Terry added, gesturing toward Steven.

"This is my grandson, Steven," said Henry, who did not mention that Steven was Terry's son. Ashley and Henry spoke about this during car ride and agreed that Ashley would be the one to break the news. Steven knew to keep quiet and follow his mom's lead.

"Welcome, Steven. I'm Terry," Terry said.

After removing Henry and Steven's luggage from the trunk of
the car, Terry led them to the house.

"It's nice to meet you finally, Mr. Benson, after all this time.
Ashley talked about you and her mother so much," Terry said.
"I just could not understand why she would never call you; she
had said it has been too long and she was ashamed of leaving
in the first place. I had to respect my wife's wishes so didn't
intervene behind her back, though I wanted to. I hope you
understand."

"I do, Terry. I had a wife I loved dearly, and would have done
the same as you had she been in the same position Ashley was
in; respect her wishes," Henry said.

Terry knew all along that there was more to the story but never
pressed Ashley to tell him. He felt if she wanted him to know,
she would tell him when she believed the time was right.

"You must both be very hungry after the long flight from Los
Angeles," Terry said. "Ashley, should we take Henry and
Steven to a restaurant, order pizza for delivery, or would you
like for me to prepare a dinner while you and your dad sit, talk,
and catch up?"

"Daddy, what would you like?" Ashley asked.

"I'd like to not have you or Terry not go through all the fuss
spending time in the kitchen. I'm happy to buy a restaurant
dinner or pay for pizza delivery," said Henry. "Which do you
prefer, Ashley."

"I want what Steven wants. What do want, Steven?" Ashley asked.

"Pizza, please," Steven said.

"Please? My, what a well-mannered and polite young man you are, Steven," Terry said. "I bet your parents are very proud of you."

Steven did not know what to say. He looked at Henry as if to ask for help. Henry deflected and brought the conversation back to dinner.

"Then pizza it is!" said Henry.

Terry asked Steven and Henry what they liked about their pizza and placed the order. "So, what shall we do until the pizza arrives?" Terry said. "You've been cooped up on an airplane for hours. Should we take a walk together and have you stretch your legs? Let Steven burn some energy? We have about 45 minutes until the pizza arrives," Terry said.

"None of the above," Ashley said, pointing at the couch instead of the chair Terry was accustomed to sitting in. "Terry, I need you to have a seat; there's something important that I need to tell you."

Terry took a seat on the couch, and Ashley sat next to him and called Steven to her side. "Terry, Steven is your son," said Ashley. "Steven is the surprise my dad told me about on the phone when we talked yesterday.

Terry was in a state of shock. He couldn't believe Ashley had kept this from him. He knew it would not be proper to ask Ashley the details in front of Steven. He was happy to find out he had a son but knew he couldn't show the real emotions he was now feeling about this secret that had been kept from him. This just wasn't the time.

Terry realized that this moment would be a seminal moment is young Steven's life; what happened next would be seared in his memory for the rest of his life. This was his son, so Terry wanted the best for Steven.

"Wow! Steven! My boy! Welcome home, Steven. Welcome home, son!" Terry said, mustering all the excitement in his voice that he could. "I love you, Steven! Let's have a family hug!"

Terry pulled Ashley and Steven close and hugged them tightly. Ashely began crying. After years of trying to have a baby of their own with no success, Terry was now a father. Ashley was unable to conceive a child; she considered her being barren as God's punishment for giving up Steven.

After hugging, Terry placed a hand on each of Steven's shoulders and said, "Well, now. Today is, without a doubt, the best day of my life! What a wonderful surprise!"

The family enjoyed the evening together eating pizza and playing board games. Steven did not say much. He was nervous. At bedtime, Terry told Steven that tomorrow is going to be a very special day, tucked him into bed, and kissed him good night.

Terry and Ashley had quite a conversation in their bed before going to sleep. "Now what?" Terry asked. "Now, what do we do? Steven is our son. He cannot go back to California. He needs to stay here, where he belongs."

"I'll talk to my dad tomorrow about everything," Ashley said. "But not in front of Steven, of course."

"Of course not," said Terry. "Don't tell your father about our money problems. He may not allow Steven to stay here with us. One way or another, we'll make ends meet, even if that means my finding a second job.

Ashley fell asleep quickly. Terry did not sleep at all that night. He was scheduled to be at work when the auto-parts store opened at 8am but knew he had to take the day off, something he could not afford to do, and spend it with Steven. Ashley was always in and out of work. She had no marketable skill so took on housecleaning jobs as they became available.

Making rent every month was always a close call. Some months, they were a few days late and incurred a late-payment penalty, which further strained the budget. The thought of not having enough money to support a son weighed heavily on Terry's mind, and this thought kept him up all night.

The next morning, Terry informed Ashley that he would let his boss know what happened as soon as he got to work, ask for the day off, and beg to be rescheduled on an off day later in the week so they would not lose out on a day's pay. His boss was not happy about Terry asking for the day off without prior notice since that meant the store would be short-handed on a morning when the supply truck arrived. Without Terry, nobody would be there to unload the truck and restock shelves.

Terry called Ashley shortly after arriving from work to break the bad news that he needed to stay at work until his boss found an employee with the day off willing to come in and replace him. Around noon, Terry called home again, telling Ashley he was on his way home and asking her to prepare a picnic lunch so he and Steven could eat while playing at the park together.

Henry cooked breakfast for Ashley and Steven while Terry was at work. They kept the conversation light. Ashley asked Steven plenty of questions about his life at the house in Cambria and playing at the seashore. She asked him what he liked to do and found out he enjoyed Superman comic books.

"Well now, Steven. That settles it. Looks like we'll have to go into town and see if we can't find some Superman stuff for you," Ashley said. "Maybe a poster or two and some toys, too."

After breakfast, Ashley suggested they walk to the park that was around the corner to let Steven play. Henry agreed that it was a great idea; he knew Ashley wanted to talk about some things that would be better said not in front of Steven.

While Steven ran around the playground making new friends, Ashley and Henry sat together on a park bench watching Steven play.

"Daddy, we need to talk about some things," Ashley said.

"I figured as such," Henry replied.

"Why, daddy? Why? Why were you so hard on me when I was a teenager?" Ashley asked. "I've been waiting all these years to know the answer to the question that caused me to run away from the home where I had a dad and mom that I loved so much."

Henry told Ashley the story of finding the letter she wrote years earlier, after he arrived in Cambria. "I never wanted to make you feel caged. I was overly protective of you because I loved you so much," Henry said. "I saw right through Bill. I knew he wasn't good for you. I'm sorry I didn't let you go out as much as you wanted to, but I was afraid that you would get hurt. I loved you too much, I guess."

"You were right, daddy," Ashley said. "As soon as I left home with Bill, my life went downhill. Once he me isolated, he began treating me badly. I started drinking and couldn't stop."

"Ashley, honey, how about we let the past stay in the past, and move forward from here," said Henry.

Ashley agreed. The only events from the past she wanted to hear about were how her mom died and how Henry found Steven. Henry explained everything. Then he reached for his wallet, took out $100, and gave it to Ashley.

"I wasn't eavesdropping, Ashley. The house was quiet and Terry was speaking a bit louder than he should have been. I guess he wasn't used to having other people in the house," Henry began. "I know that things are tight moneywise for the two of you. Take this so you have money to spend on Steven today. We'll talk later about finances when Terry is out with Steven later today."

Ashley took the money, hugged her dad, and began crying. "I love you, daddy," she said.

Just then, Steven ran up to his mom and grandpa and noticed his mom crying. He looked at Henry with a confused look on his face. Henry knew exactly what to say to the boy.

"Not to worry, Steven. They're tears of joy," he said. "How about we head out and get you some toys to play with at home."

Steven smiled and nodded in approval. The three left the park and walked to a nearby shopping plaza where Ashley bought Steven an ice cream, a Superman cape and comic book, and a cowboy hat and toy pistols with holsters. Steven wore his cape on the walk home, pretending to be Superman. When they got home, he put on his new cowboy hat and placed the pistols in the holsters that hung around his waist.

Near noon, Ashley prepared a picnic lunch for Steven and Terry, who was set to be home at any minute. While Ashley was in the kitchen, Henry had a conversation with Steven, letting him know that it would make his mom and dad very happy if he would call them "mom" and "dad" when he spoke to them.

"Steven, you've always wanted a mom and dad, and now you have a mom and dad," said Henry. "Understand, Steven?"

"I understand, grandpa," Steven said.

Ashley came in from the kitchen with the packed picnic basket and said, "Steven, your father will be home any minute now and will be taking you to the park. I've packed a lunch for the two of you. Grandpa told me that you like peanut butter and strawberry jelly sandwiches, so that's what I made for you. Okay?"

Steven looked at Henry, who nodded. And then Steven looked at his mom and said, "Okay, mom. Thank you."

Hearing Steven finally call her "mom" made Ashley begin crying again, prompting Steven to innocently say, "You sure do cry a lot, ma'am, I mean, mom."

His comment made Henry and Ashley begin laughing. "Tears of joy, Steven, my beautiful son, these are tears of joy!" Ashley said.

"You sure do cry a lot of tears of joy," Steven said.

"That's because I'm so happy to finally have you in my life, Steven," Ashley said.

Just then, Terry walked in the door. "Where's my little boy? I'm taking him to the park."

"Yay! Daddy's home!" said Ashley. "There's your little boy, and here's your picnic basket."

"Where? I don't see him," said Terry

"Right here, daddy," said Steven, standing a few feet right in front of his dad.

"You're not fooling me. You're not Steven; you're Superman. Hello, Superman. Have you seen my son, Steven?" Terry said.

"I'm not Superman; I'm Steven," Steven said while laughing.

"No, you're Superman. Say, Superman, will you go the park with me and help me find my son, Steven?" Terry asked.

Steven decided to play along with the game of make-believe, and said, "Okay. I'll help you find Steven."

"Great! Let's go! We'll see you later Mr. Benson. You too, Ashley. And when we come back home, not to worry, Ashley. We'll have our son, Steven, with us. Superman is going to help me find him and save the day," said Terry.

"Don't forget your picnic basket," Ashley. "But first have a look inside before you walk out the door."

Ashley said this so Henry would notice the $40 and note she placed inside. The note let Terry know that the money is a gift from her father so Terry would have money to spend on Steven.

Several hours later when Terry and Steven arrived home, Steven was wearing a Cincinnati Reds baseball uniform and had a baseball bat, glove, and baseball. It was clear that Terry and Steven had a great afternoon together.

The next morning, Terry took Steven to the park to teach him how to hit a baseball. Ashley and Henry watched from a park bench and reminisced about Ashley's childhood. Though

Steven called Terry and Ashley "dad" and "mom," he stayed by Henry's side when they were at home.

"Terry and I want to have a close relationship with Steven, but he stays next to you unless Terry or I call him to us," said Ashley. "I want that to change, daddy. How do I do that? Terry and I can't keep buying him whatever he wants; that will spoil him and make him not appreciate what he has."

"Being a mom means more than just giving birth," Henry began. "Being a mother and father means raising a child, caring for them when their sick, spending time together talking. It's going to take time, Ashley."

Henry purchased one-way tickets for him and Steven. He was unsure how things would develop in Ohio and wanted to be free to leave whenever he wanted to. Things were going well, but he knew he could not stay longer than a few weeks. And there was no way he would ever leave Steven in Ohio with Ashley and Terry, no matter how well they accepted and treated their son.

"How much longer do you plan on staying in Ohio, daddy?" Ashley asked.

"I don't have a set return date in mind, honey," Henry replied. "But I know that Steven and I will need to return home in a week or so."

"Daddy, Terry and I were talking and we'd like for you to leave Steven here with us," said Ashley.

"That's not going happen, honey. I'm sorry," Henry said. "That wouldn't be fair to Steven. I told you that he bounced around from home to home until he came to live with me last year. He finally has stability in his life. We've bonded. Steven trusts me. You and Terry need to earn his trust. That's not going to happen over a few weeks."

Ashley felt a little angry, but did not let it show. She understood her dad was right. Besides, she willingly gave up Steven. She knew she should be thankful that her son ended up with her dad, was being raised in a good home, and was well-cared for and happy.

"How do Terry and I bond with Steven when he lives 2,000 miles away?" Ashley protested.

"Frequent visits," Henry said. "School starts in a few weeks. I can fly you and Terry out for the four-day Thanksgiving weekend, and then when Steven has a two-week Christmas break, we'll bring you out again. Then there's a one-week Easter break from school, and soon after that, a three-month summer vacation."

"I don't know if I'm able to go so long in between visits not seeing my son," Ashley said.

"I agree that Steven needs to live with his mom and dad, but not until the time is right," Henry said. "That's the way that it is. I have legal custody and will agree to have Steven live with you when I believe the time is right."

After staying for another week, Henry and Steven returned home. It was just as Henry said it would be; Steven was sad to say good-bye to his parents, but glad to be returning home to Cambria with his granddad. On the flight home, Steven asked Henry when he would see his mom and dad again. Henry told him that his parents would be visiting Cambria during Thanksgiving break, in about three months.

Henry knew he had to watch Steven closely when they got back home, looking for signs of depression, signaling that he developed a strong bond with his mom and dad. Steven was just fine. He was the same happy child that he was before going to Ohio. He was excited every Sunday evening when Henry called Ashley and Terry so he could talk to them for about 30 minutes but never questioned not living with them. His grandpa and grandpa's house was his family and his home.

Chapter 13

The Plan

Good thing for Henry that he had Carol to talk with about his dilemma. Carol was a good listener. She never told Henry what he should do; she only asked a lot of questions in hope that Henry would come to the right answers on his own.

Understanding that he can't take his money with him when he dies, and he wasn't getting any younger, Henry decided to purchase the cottage next door for Terry and Ashley to live in, rent free. He always wanted the cottage back in the family anyway.

Henry knew Terry was happy working in the auto parts store. The problem was that Cambria did not have an auto-parts store in town. The nearest parts store was 30 miles away in Paso Robles. Henry decided to purchase the vacant building across the street from Glen Cliff's Ice Cream store and have his attorney get the ball rolling on filing paperwork with the state, county, and city to open an auto parts store.

Like not telling Ashley and Terry about Steven, Henry kept his plan a surprise. He would let them in on it when they came for their Thanksgiving visit. He did broach the subject of living in Cambria on a private phone call with Ashley while Terry was at work and Steven at school.

Ashley loved the sea, missed Cambria, and wanted to be near Steven. Moving back to Cambria sounded like a great idea. All she needed to do was convince her husband, which she began doing when he came home from work. Terry was uncomfortable quitting his job and moving across the country without having a new job waiting on him, but was willing to relocate. He did not have any ties in Akron since his mom and dad died many years ago. Moving to Cambria was an easy sell.

Ashley shared the good news with her dad but told him Terry's one condition: he would take a leave of absence from work, and if he couldn't find a job within a few weeks, they were moving back to Ohio. Henry called Ashley the next day and lied to his daughter so she would tell Terry what he needed to hear without her willingly lying to him.

"Ashley, great news," said Henry. "I have a few job offers waiting on Henry when he gets here. He can work for Carol at the Inn until he finds something else in town, or he can commute to Paso Robles five days a week to work in an auto-parts store there. He'll have Carol to thank for that too. She pulled a few strings."

"Wow, daddy! Wow! I'll tell him as soon as he walks in the door after work!" Ashley said. "Or would you like for me to call you so you can tell him?"

"You tell him. Cross-country phone calls are expensive except on Sundays," Henry said. "Have Terry put in notice at work, I'll talk to him on Sunday, and then Steven and I will be seeing you in a few weeks."

Terry and Ashley arrived the day before Thanksgiving. Henry wanted to make things easy for them by picking them up at Los Angeles Airport. Ashley and Terry wanted to make things easy on Henry, so they stayed overnight in Los Angeles, took a taxi to Van Nuys Airport the next morning, hopped on a Cessna and flew into San Luis Obispo where Henry would pick them up.

Henry's dream was coming true. His family would be together again in a few weeks. His began to feel sad that Victoria was not alive to see it happen, but then he remembered the morning after his dream and the supernatural experience he had. He knew Victoria would be there in spirit.

The big day finally arrived. Ashley was beside herself with glee. It was the happiest day of her life. Soon she would be home in Cambria with a husband she loved, her father who had forgiven her, and the beautiful son she thought about often. Terry, like Steven before him, lived his entire life in Ohio and had never seen the ocean. Ashley talked the entire trip, repeating the same stories over and over numerous times. Terry found it cute and amusing; he was happy for his wife, and excited about being a father.

In confidence and to ease any worry, Henry told Ashley that he had plenty of money, so she and Terry would not need to worry about making ends meet on the meager wage he would earn working at Carol's Inn or the parts store in Paso Robles. He asked her to keep the information to herself because blood is thicker than water and his finances were none of Terry's business.

Henry wanted Terry to be authentically concerned for his daughter's and grandson's well-being and not be influenced by knowing he would be financially secure as long as they stay married. After all, Terry was stepping out on his wife when he met Ashley, so Henry had a certain level of dislike and distrust of Terry. If Terry ever did that to his little girl, there would be a price to pay – every penny of family money.

Henry had a clause put into the contract transferring ownership of the parts store and building that noted if Terry was unfaithful to Ashley, or if they got divorced, the building and business ownership reverted to Ashley. Terry's name was left off the cottage property title completely; the cottage would be owned outright by Ashley from the get-go.

The day arrived. The sun shone brightly through clear, blue skies. Carol accompanied Henry and Steven to San Luis Obispo Airport to pick up Ashley and Terry. Henry hadn't told Ashley about Carol becoming more than just a friend. That news would wait until Terry and Ashley settled in. He was also unsure when he would tell them about buying the cottage for them to live in and the auto-parts store he bought for Henry.

Henry, Carol, and Steven arrived at the airport nearly an hour early so they grabbed a bite to eat at the airport diner. About 10 minutes before Ashley's plane was scheduled to land, an announcement came over the loud speaker.

"Ladies and gentlemen, your attention please. Your attention. Fred's Air Service Flight 64 from Van Nuys Airport will be landing five minutes early, and passengers will disembark at

Gate 4. Fred's Air Service Flight 64 from Van Nuys Airport will be landing five minutes early. Passengers will disembark at Gate 4. Thank you."

This was it. Ashley was coming home for good. Henry looked at Carol, took a deep breath, and said, "Let's go make our way to Gate 4. Ready, Steven?"

Steven nodded. Carol smiled and took Steven's hand, and they began the short walk to Gate 4, which was nothing more than a sign hung above a door in the only building at the airport. A small plane could be seen approaching the airfield from the west. It was a blue and white Cessna flown with a "Fred's Air Service" decal on the fuselage, piloted by Fred Simpson, another pilot with jet fighter combat time in the Korean War now using his talents for peaceful means.

The plane landed and taxied to park about 50 yards away from Gate 4. It came to a stop and Fred shut down the plane's single-engine propeller. A young man wearing coveralls dashed to the plane, placed wooden wheel chocks at the front and back of the wheels, signaled Fred with a thumbs-up, and then opened the plane's door.

Ashley stepped out first, followed by Terry, then Fred, who had something in his hand. The young man opened a small cargo door and grabbed luggage. The four of them then walked to Gate 4 and entered the terminal.

"Daddy! I'm home, daddy! I'm finally home!" said Ashley, giving her dad a hug before turning to Steven, hugging him and saying, "Steven! I love you, Steven!"

Terry extended his hand and said, "Mr. Benson, thank you for all you're doing for us. We don't plan on inconveniencing you and we'll find a place to stay as soon as possible."

Ashley recognized Carol and the two hugged. "Welcome, sport," Carol said, using the pet name she called Ashley when she was a little girl. "This must be Terry. Hi Terry, I'm Carol."

"Hello, Carol," said Terry. "I owe you a debt of gratitude for pulling strings and finding me a job. I won't let you down, ma'am."

"Ma'am sham. Call me Carol," she said. "And I know you won't let me down. If I thought there was a chance of that, I wouldn't have arranged employment for you. Henry speaks highly of you."

Hearing that his father-in-law had confidence in him and spoke well of his character made Terry very happy. He turned to Henry and said, "Thank you, sir. That means a lot."

Henry was just fine with Terry calling him "sir," or "Mr. Benson," until Terry proved himself. Henry went out on a limb for his son-in-law and risked a lot by purchasing a building and paying to having it stocked with auto-parts.

"Oh, I almost forgot. Daddy, this is Fred, our amazing pilot," said Ashley.

"Pleased to meet you, Henry," said Fred, who turned to Steven and said, "And you must be Steven. I've heard a lot of good things about you. This is for you, young man. Enjoy. It was a pleasure meeting you folks. Ashley, welcome home and best of luck. My offer stands. You have my card. Call me when you're ready. Jimmy, carry the luggage to their car and then come on back and start maintenance on my plane."

Fred handed Steven a scale-model replica of his airplane, complete with Fred's Air Service decals and tail number. It even had a pilot in the cockpit that looked like old Fred. As everyone walked to the old '49 Plymouth, Steven held the toy plane at arm's length, made a motor noise, and pretended it was flying alongside him.

"What was that all about?" Henry asked Ashley. "Why did Fred give you his card and tell you to call when you're ready? Ready for what? Do you plan on leaving soon?"

Ashley began laughing. "No, daddy. Of course not," she said. "Fred said he would be happy to take Steven on a plane ride sometime."

"Whew! That was close. You had me worried," said Henry.

"Daddy, I'm not going anywhere. You're stuck with me for life!" said Ashley.

Ashley did not say a word on the drive home, except to comment, "It's just as beautiful as it was when I was a girl." After all these years of wanting to return home, Ashley was now mere minutes away. Henry detoured down Cambria's Main Street so Ashley could see the old sights and bring back great memories, and Terry could take them in and make them for the first time.

"Main Street changed, Daddy," Ashley said. "There are a few more bed and breakfasts and antique shops. Look! Glen Cliff's Ice Cream is still here! Oh, daddy, let's stop in! I want one of those strawberry double-scoop ice cream cones you used to buy for me when I was a little girl!"

"You like the strawberry ice cream too, mom? That's my favorite too! Grandpa took me here the first day we came to Cambria!" Steven said.

"Oh, look! Across the street. It's Mr. Higgins' Antique shop, and he still has the wishing well!" said Ashley. "I want to go there with my ice cream and throw a penny in, just like when I was a little girl. Do you remember taking me there, Daddy?"

"Grandpa took me to the wishing well, too, the first day we came here!" said Steven.

"What did you wish for?" Ashley asked as Henry parked the car.

"I wished I would have a mom and a dad," Steven said. "And it came true."

Ashley looked at Steven and began crying, again. She opened her car door, took Steven by the hand, and dashed across the street to the wishing well.

"You better go along with them, Terry," Henry said. "Steven wished for a mom AND a dad. That's you."

Terry smiled at Henry, nodded, and said, "Yes sir. I'm on my way."

Henry looked at Carol and began crying. "Looks like everybody's wish came true, Mr. Benson," Carol said. "Let's go join them."

"No, Miss Hanson. Let's stay here, watch, and take it all in," Henry said.

From inside the store, Mr. Higgins saw Steven with two adults he had never seen before. He came outside and said, "Well howdy, young man. Who do we have her with……Ashley? Ashley Benson? Say it ain't so! Is it you?"

"Hi, Mr. Higgins! It's me, Ashley! But now I'm Ashley Mars. And this is my husband, Terry Mars," Ashley said.

"Pleased to meet you, Terry Mars," Mr. Higgins said, shaking Terry's hand. "I hear you're moving back home. Welcome home, Ashley."

"Thank you, Mr. Higgins," said Ashley.

"Now once you make a wish and toss a penny into the wishing well, come on inside and see me. Do you hear?" said Mr. Higgins.

Ashley nodded, reached into her purse, and grabbed three pennies. Mr. Higgins noticed Carol and Henry across the street, standing by the car, watching. Mr. Higgins gave Henry a thumbs-up and waved. The he hollered, "The family will be back your way in a few minutes. I asked them to come inside for a minute."

Henry nodded and mouthed, "Thank you." After Terry, Ashley, and Steve made a wish and tossed a penny into the wishing well, they went inside Mr. Higgins' Antiques.

"Now then, young lady, a welcome home gift is in order, so take a look around and pick something out real nice for yourself, and no arguing. I insist," said Mr. Higgins. "I insist."

Ashley took Steven by the hand and browsed around for several minutes while Mr. Higgins engaged in small talk with Terry, getting to know him. A few minutes later, Ashley and Steven approached the counter. Ashley picked out a wooden mini-wishing well customers made and donated to the store for Mr. Higgins to sell at 100 percent profit.

"I'll take this," she said.

"Sold!" said Mr. Higgggins. "In fact, grab another one for Steven here, too."

On their way out, Ashley and Steven gave Mr. Higgins a big hug and told him that he could expect to see a lot more of them from now on. Mr. Higgins shook Terry's hand and bid them goodbye. The Mars family crossed the street to join Henry and Carol and go into Glen Cliff's Ice Cream shop for their double scoop strawberry ice cream cones.

Henry noticed that Terry had an uncomfortable look on his face and inquired if everything was okay. Terry told Henry that everything was fine, just overcome with emotion about beginning a new life with his son in a wonderful town.

Ashley was excited to see all the cows in the field on the way home. She rolled down her window and asked Henry to pull over so she could look for a minute. When she heard the cows moo, she told Steven that the cows were saying, "Welcome Home, Ashley!" This made Steven laugh.

"Mom, cows can't talk," Steven said.

"Sure, they can," said Ashley.

"No, mom. All cows can say is 'Mooooooo,'" Steven said.

"It may sound like all they're saying is 'Moooooo' if you don't understand cow language," laughed Ashley. "When I was a little girl, I used to come down here and talk to them, and they taught me how to speak and understand cow. Right, daddy?"

"Right you are, sweetheart," Henry said.

"I'll tell you what, Steven. Tomorrow, I'll bring you down here, introduce you to the cows and teach you cow language," Ashley said. "Let's go, daddy. I can't wait to get home. Bye, cows! Did you hear that, Steven? They cows are saying, 'See ya' later, Ashley. Welcome home!'"

Steven thought his mom talking to the cows was the funniest thing he had ever heard. It was a real kick in the pants. He laughed about it all the way home. Then, a few minutes later, they were home.

"Look! The rose bushes are still here! Remember when we planted rose bushes together, daddy, and mommy watched us from the porch swing?" Ashley said.

"Ofcourse I do, honey," Henry said.

Henry parked the car, and everybody got out except Ashley. Henry asked her if everything is okay. Ashley was staring at the porch swing.

"Daddy, don't think I've lost my mind, but……" began Ashley before pausing.

"But what, honey?" said Henry.

"Daddy, in my mind I can see mommy sitting on the porch swing, gently swinging like she loved to do," Ashley said.

"You're not crazy, honey. Mom is here in spirit. You see her spirit, sweetheart," said Henry, who began crying.

"Boy, oh boy. This family sure cries a lot," said Steven. "I know, I know. Tears of joy."

Ashley was spellbound as she stood looking at the old house. It was exactly as she remembered. The guardian angels on the front door made her cry more. Terry carried the luggage into the house and Henry walked him upstairs to the room where he an Ashley would be staying – Ashley's old room.

When they came back downstairs, Carol mentioned that she should be going and asked Henry to drive her back to the Inn. Henry protested and asked Carol to stay for a bit. Carol insisted it was time for the family to have time alone. Judging by Ashley's silence – not asking Carol to stay – Henry sensed that Ashley wanted some time with just herself, Terry, Steven, and her dad.

Carol hugged Ashley good bye and told her that she would see her soon, and then went outside to the car. Henry told Steven to show Terry where the firewood was kept and help his dad start a fire while he was gone. The fire was started and the three sat down, enjoying the warmth.

Ashley, like her father earlier, noticed Terry looked uncomfortable as if something was weighing on him. She inquired, and Terry, looking at Steven, insisted nothing was the matter. She took this as a hint that he did not want to discuss whatever was on his mind in front of young Steven. Just then, the phone rang. It was Mr. Higgins calling.

"Hello," Ashley answered.

"Ashley, hi. I need to talk with your dad," said Mr. Higgins.

"Oh, hi, Mr. Higgins. Thank you again for the gifts," Ashley said. "My dad isn't home; he's taking Carol back to the Inn and should be right back."

"Did Terry talk to you? Did he tell you about our conversation?" Mr. Higgins asked.

"No, he hasn't said a word," Ashley answered. "What happened? What's wrong? Terry looks troubled. Both my dad and I notice."

“Good grief, dear,” said Mr. Higgins. “I need to go. I need to meet your dad at the Inn before he leaves. I messed up and owe him quite the apology. I’m afraid I’ve made a mess of things. I’m sure your dad will talk to you when he returns. Good bye, Ashley.”

Mr. Higgins hung up, and Ashley went to sit beside Terry.

“That was Mr. Higgins on the phone,” Ashley said.

Terry turned to Steven and said, “Son, how about going upstairs to your room for a few minutes. Your mom and I need to have an adult conversation. I’ll call you down when we’re done.”

“Did I do something wrong, dad,” Steven asked.

“No, you did nothing wrong,” said Terry. “Now run along. We only need a few minutes.”

Steven did as he was instructed. While he was upstairs, out of earshot, Terry told Ashley what Mr. Higgins told him, but shouldn’t have. While this conversation occurred, Henry happened to be driving down Main Street and passing Mr. Higgins’ store. Mr. Higgins had just walked outside on his way to his car to drive to Carol’s Inn and meet Henry. When Mr. Higgins saw Henry, he waved frantically and hollered to get Henry’s attention.

“That doesn’t look good,” Henry said to Carol. “Something must have happened.”

Henry pulled over, parked, and got out of the car. "Ray, is everything Okay?" Henry asked.

"I'm afraid not," said Ray Higgins. "I messed up, Henry. I messed up really bad. I owe you an explanation and an apology. Please, come inside so we can have a talk. It's important."

"I'll wait here while you two men talk," Carol said. "Take all the time you need, Henry."

Henry and Mr. Higgins went into the store and Mr. Higgins walked Henry to his office in the back of the building.

"Sit down, Henry," said Mr. Higgins. "Henry, I'm sorry. I had no idea that buying the cottage and the vacant store to turn into an auto parts shop was a surprise. When Ashley was here earlier, she and Steven were browsing around and Terry and I were talking by the register. I opened my big mouth. I'm sorry Henry. I can't tell you how sorry I am. I've really blown it for you, my old friend. And how."

"Ray, it's not your fault; it's mine. I didn't tell you it was a surprise," said Henry. "Forget about it. Water under the bridge, my old friend. Water under the bridge."

"Geeee, Henry. You sure are being gracious and understanding over it all. Tell me how I can make it up to you, and I'll do it," said Mr. Higgins.

"As I said, Ray. You can forget all about it. That's repayment enough. You didn't know," Henry said.

"You're a fine man, Henry. I'm honored to call you my friend," said Mr. Higgins.

"We go back a long way, Ray. We served together in France in World War I. We're friends for life, Ray," said Henry. "I'm sure we'll be laughing about the entire ordeal before too long."

"Help yourself to whatever you need on your way out," said Mr. Higgins.

"I'll have none of that. I can pay for whatever I need," said Henry. "Let's forget about it and move on."

Henry and Mr. Higgins shook hands, and that was that. Neither of them ever mentioned it again. When Henry got back to his car, he told Carol what had happened.

"I'm sure you told Ray to forget about it," said Carol.

"Indeed, I did, Carol," said Henry. "It was an honest mistake."

Henry dropped off Carol at the Inn and drove back home. The cat was out of the bag. Henry told himself that some things are meant to be, and perhaps it was for the better that Ashley knew what he had done for her. After all, knowing that she and Terry had a place to live and Terry had an income waiting for him should relieve any stress they were feeling over thinking about whether or not the ersatz job Carol lined up would be to his liking.

By the time Henry pulled into his driveway, Terry had finished telling Ashley the news and Steven had rejoined them downstairs. When they heard Henry's old '49 Plymouth pull up, they all walked outside to greet him. Terry hugged Henry.

"Thank you! Thank you, sir," said Terry while embracing his father-in-law. "I don't know how to thank you. Words are not enough, Mr. Benson. I'm floored. Absolutely floored. I know how much you love your daughter, but I'm essentially a stranger. I won't let you down, sir. You have my solemn word. I don't expect any handouts. I believe in earning what I have."

"You are very welcome, Terry," said Henry. "Give it all 100 percent and I'll be satisfied. Your effort is what matters."

"Sir," Terry said. "There is one thing."

"What's that?" Henry asked.

"With your permission, sir, I would like to call you, 'Dad.' Is that okay?" asked Terry.

"Sure thing, son," Henry said.

The two hugged once again, and then Terry began crying. Next, it was Ashley's turn to hug her dad, say thank you, and begin crying.

"Oh, daddy! I love you! Terry won't let you down. He's a good man and a hard worker," said Ashley. "You'll see. I wouldn't be married to him if he wasn't."

Everybody went inside to sit by the fire together. Ashley was anxious to move into the cottage right away. Terry did not dare mention moving in. He committed himself to letting Ashley take the lead so he would not appear to be overly consumed with freebies. After sitting and talking about what needed to be done to open the parts store, Ashley volunteered to cook dinner. She prepared one of her dad's favorite meals – steak and potatoes, corn on the cob, and a salad.

After dinner, Ashley asked if they could all walk to the cottage and have a look. Henry agreed. The cottage was not quite ready for move-in. Painters were scheduled to arrive on Monday, followed by a furniture delivery the next day. There were no kitchen items – plates, utensils, pots, pans, etc. – or bedding. Henry planned on taking Ashley shopping so she could choose whatever she wanted.

While at the cottage, Henry pulled Ashley aside to give her news she would not like, perhaps. "One thing, sweetheart," Henry began. "Steven will stay living with me for the time being. Once he's comfortable with you and Terry, he can move in with you. I'm not giving up legal custody just yet. Understand?"

Ashley was disappointed but didn't show it. "I understand, daddy. You're looking out for his best interest is all. Do you know what I wished for at the wishing well earlier today?"

"What's that, honey? What did you wish for?" Henry asked.

"I wished that Terry would make enough money for us to buy this cottage so we could be near you. And it came true!" said Ashley, hugging her dad. "Let's all go down to the seashore before the sun sets. Terry's never set foot in the ocean!"

Down at the beach, Terry was all smiles. He enjoyed being at the sea. He had never smelled the ocean's salty air or touched its salt water. Ashley and Steven looked for seashells while Terry and Henry talked. Near sunset, they made their way back up the bluff to Henry's house. It was time to settle in for the night. Tomorrow would be a busy day.

The next morning, Ashley and Terry were woken up by the smell of bacon and eggs cooking in a frying pan. When they came downstairs for breakfast, they found an envelope with their names on it sitting on the dining room table. Inside were the keys to the cottage and a card that read: "Welcome home! Love, Dad."

Over breakfast, Terry said, "Dad, Ashley, and I talked about a few things last night. We cannot accept the cottage outright. I insist that we pay you rent."

Henry refused Terry's offer. "No, son. The cottage is a wedding present."

Terry looked at Ashley, who gave her husband a look that a wife gives her husband, her message requiring no words. Her look said not to argue with her dad about it because it wouldn't make him happy. Terry knew better than to cross his wife.

"Thank you, dad. In that case, I insist that I pay you rent on the auto parts store then," Terry said. "Will you accept that?"

"I'll consider it and let you know when I decide," Henry said.

Terry looked at Ashley again, who was smiling. This told Terry to shut his mouth about it, accept Henry's answer, and wait for Henry's answer, whenever that time would be.

Ashley changed the subject and began talking about memories of when she was a little girl eating breakfast, looking out the window at the sea below. She told Steven about seeing ships passing by and seagulls by the hundreds circling above the shoreline, looking for food. On foggy mornings, she imagined there were pirate ships hidden in the fog, coming ashore to bury their treasure.

Steven told his mom about looking for the pirate's treasure with his grandpa but still hadn't found anything. Terry just listened. After breakfast, Terry, Ashley, and Steven cleaned up the kitchen and washed the dishes and then it was time to drive into town and look at the soon-to-be auto-parts store.

Since it was a Saturday, Steven had no school, so was able to spend the day with his parents and grandpa. There was a sign in the store's window that said "SOLD." And another sign that read: "AUTO PARTS STORE COMING SOON."

Henry handed Terry the key and said, "Here you go, son. Open it up and let's have a look."

The store was empty. Henry told Terry he made appointments with several salesmen on Monday to meet them at the shop throughout the day. The salesmen represented several different competing companies. Some sold shelving, others signage. Some sold parts, and others all the non-auto-part items needed to run a store, like cash registers and administrative supplies.

Henry told Terry it was best to go through larger wholesalers to get the store everything it needed to become open for business. After that, he suggested Terry buy whatever he could locally, from businesses along Main Street, and everything else from wholesalers.

On the following day, Tuesday, they had an appointment at the bank to set-up the business banking account. This was followed by an appointment with Sally Caspar, who owned an accounting business in town. She would be handling the accounting and payroll for employees.

"Now for the big question, Terry," Henry said. "You need to come up with a name for your auto-parts store by Monday."

"I've got the perfect name in mind, dad," Terry said. "Benson's Auto Parts. I'd be honored to have your family name grace my business."

"Terry, I appreciate that, but no. I can't agree to that. This is your shop, not mine," said Henry.

"Fair enough," Terry said. Looking at Steven, he said, "How about 'Mars and Son Auto Parts'?"

"'Mars and Son Auto Parts.' That has a nice ring to it. Think on it over the weekend, and if you still like it come Monday morning then I think you should go with it," said Henry, who turned his attention to Steven and said, "How about some ice cream, Steven?"

Henry and his family walked to Glen Cliff's Ice Cream shop, and on the way, they crossed paths with Mary DeFaria, Ashley's old friend from high school.

"Mary? Mary DeFaria?" said Ashley.

"Ashley?! Ashley Benson?!" Mary replied.

The two hugged. They hadn't seen one another in over a decade. Mary was with her son, Daniel, who happened to be Steven's elementary school classmate.

"I'm not a DeFaria anymore. Do you remember Billie Jones from 10th-grade algebra?" Mary asked.

"Ofcourse I do," said Ashley.

"Well, I'm Mrs. Jones now," said Mary.

"Where is Billie?" Ashley asked.

"He's working today. He works at Paso Robles Auto Parts in Paso Robles. He hates the commute," said Mary.

Ashley introduced Terry and Mary, but said nothing about their now-owned soon-to-be-opened parts store. She knew that was something she and Terry had to talk about first. Ashley invited Mary and Daniel to enjoy some ice cream with them, which they gladly did.

Ashley and Mary got caught up with one another's life while enjoying their frozen treats. Afterwards, Henry suggested they take the boys to the park to let them play and burn energy while the adults talked. After an hour or so at the park, it was nearing lunch time. Henry suggested going to Mustache Pete's Place, his treat, including Mary and Daniel. He wanted Mary and Ashley to reconnect. It would be good for Ashley to have friends in town.

On the way to Mustache Pete's Place they stopped by Mr. Higgin's store to throw a penny in the wishing well. Henry wet inside to use Mr. Higgins' phone and call Carol to invite her to join them for lunch. Henry did not drive to pick up Carol. Carol drove herself in a car she rarely used. Everything she needed was in walking distance of the Inn, and now that she and Henry were dating, whenever she had the need to go outside of town, Henry drove her.

Sitting at the table, Henry and Carol told Terry and Ashley that they had a few surprises for them, but first, Carol wanted to know what they wished for at the wishing well while she and Henry were talking on the phone.

"You know I can't share what I wish for until it happens, or else my wish is jinxed and won't come true," laughed Ashley.

"Well now, perhaps this is what you wished for," Carol said as she placed an envelope on the table. "Go ahead, Ashley, open it up."

Ashley opened the envelope and inside were car keys and paperwork. "Carol, what is this about?" Ashley asked.

"It's about that 1952 Chevy I drove here in. I don't need it, and you Terry need a car. How else is he going to get back and forth to the auto shop every day?” said Carol. “And how do you expect to get your shopping done and get Steven where he needs to be?”

“Excuse me, Ashley, Mr. Benson, sir, but enough is enough, and I need to step in and say ‘No,’” Terry said. “We cannot accept this. Enough with the handouts. I know how much you love Ashley, but I’m a man and I have my pride.”

“Fair enough,” said Carol. “Then $1,000, and I’ll take payments.”

Terry looked at Ashley, who, with a stern look as if to say, “You better agree; we desperately need a car,” nodded her head, signaling Terry that paying for the car was okay by her.

“Sold!” said Terry.

“Looks like I can share what I wished for now,” Ashley said. “A car!”

Everybody shared a good laugh, and the food was delivered. As they began to eat, Ashley reminded Carol that she said that she and her dad had a few surprises, and asked what they had in mind next.

“Honey, Carol and I are getting married this coming June,” Henry said.

“Oh, daddy!” Ashely said, as she stood up, scampered around to his side of the table and hugged her father, and then Carol. “What a great day!”

After lunch, they decided to head back home, and invited Mary and Daniel so Steven and Daniel could play for the afternoon. It was a great day for Henry's family indeed. Things could not get any better.

Chapter 14

'Til Death Do Us Part

It was Sunday morning; Henry's favorite time of day on his favorite day of the week. Henry enjoyed the peaceful stillness of Sunday mornings. On this particular Sunday morning, Henry would be taking Ashley to visit her mother's grave at the local cemetery.

Terry and Steven waited in the car so Henry and Ashley could have a special moment alone with Victoria. Henry led Ashley to a white bench beside a marble headstone. The marker had seashells engraved on the front. On it was written:

From The Sea Come Sea Shells.

And Like The Seashell Once Full Of Life,

My Lovely Wife Now Lies At Peace,

By The Side Of The Sea.

I Love You, Victoria.

Crying, Ashley laid roses from her garden at her mom's grave, and then she collapsed, crying. "I love you, mom! I love you! I'm so sorry I ran away. I'm so sorry I was not here for you," wailed Ashley.

Henry sat at the bench silently, allowing his daughter to grieve as long as she needed to. When Ashley regained her composure, she sat beside her father hugging him.

"Do you think mom forgives me, daddy?" asked Ashley.

"I don't think she forgives you; I know she forgives you," said Henry. "Mom may be gone in body, but she's with us in spirit always."

Henry told Ashley the story about his dream and his supernatural experience later that morning. He told her he once believed that believing in an afterlife, heaven, and spirits was superstitious nonsense, but now, there was no doubt in his mind that God exists, and Victoria was in heaven looking down upon the ones she loves.

On the drive home, Henry began complaining about having blurry vision. It got so bad that he pulled the car off to the side of the road and asked Terry to drive them home. As they drove through town, Henry said he was beginning to feel better. Then, just as quickly, he began seeing double and feeling dizzy. He told Ashley about it, adding that he feared something was very wrong.

Terry asked Ashley where the nearest emergency room was located, and Ashley told him that Cambria did not have one; that the nearest hospital was 30 miles away in Paso Robles.

"What do you do around here if there's a medical emergency?" Terry asked.

“We call the fire department,” said Ashley, “and they send a paramedic unit.”

Henry began complaining of a weakness on his left side and was having trouble speaking so Terry drove to the firehouse. The captain took one look at Henry, summoned his paramedics to begin aid and prepare Henry for transport. He radioed the hospital in Paso Robles, alerting them to expect a possible stroke patient within 30 minutes.

As Henry was about to be placed into the back of the ambulance, an IV was started, and then paramedics began performing CPR on Henry’s lifeless body lying on a stretcher.

“Daddy! No! Daddy!” Ashley screamed as she ran toward her father.

“Ma’am, ma’am,” said a firefighter as he stopped Ashley and held her back. “We have to let them do their job to save his life.”

The captain motioned for Terry to help console Ashley and direct her away from the scene. Steven stayed in the car watching everything. Ashley knew her father was dead. She was devastated that she didn't get a chance to get to really know her father again.

Henry was placed inside the ambulance with two paramedics who continued to perform CPR as the doors were shut. The driver started the engine, turned on the emergency lights and siren, and drove away.

Terry and Ashley returned to the car and drove to the hospital. They arrived several minutes after the ambulance and were greeted by one of the paramedics who introduced them to the emergency room physician.

"I'm sorry. Everybody did everything we could do. Your father did not make it," said the doctor. "It's best that you return home and call me so we can make arrangements for transport back to Cambria and burial."

Ashley cried the entire way back to Cambria. She told Terry to stop by the Inn to break the news to Carol. Carol was devastated. Henry died the same way her late husband did – stroke. Carol spent the day with Terry, Ashley, and Steven at Henry's house. Not much was said. When they did talk, they agreed to talk only about happy things and leave the morbid details of discussing funeral arrangements until tomorrow.

Monday was here. It was supposed to be the day Henry and Terry met with salesmen. Today, Terry would have to go it alone, or so he thought. When he showed up at the store at 8 am, Mr. Higgins was waiting for him.

"Terry, I'm sorry about Henry," said Mr. Higgins. "When Henry told me all about his plan for you and this here store, he asked me if I wouldn't mind keeping an eye out from across the street there and helping you in any way I can. So here I am. I'm here to sit with you throughout the day while salesmen make their pitch on why you should contract with them."

"Thank you, Mr. Higgins," Terry said. "I'm scared and nervous. I have no idea what I'm doing."

"I'll guide you," said Mr. Higgins. "Now go on ahead and open the shop; the first salesman should be here any minute now."

While Terry and Mr. Higgins spent the day together at Mars and Son Auto Parts planning for the future, Ashley and Carol began planning Henry's funeral. One by one, people from town showed up at Henry's house offering condolences and bringing flowers. They all had the same exact message for Ashley" "Anything you need, whenever you need it; know that I'm here for you."

What a way for Ashley to re-unite with the good people of Cambria. She was so eager to see and meet all of her dad's old friends, but this wasn't the way she wanted it to be. Everybody knew Ashley was coming back home; that was all Henry could talk about. Everyone was so happy to see a family get back together; now they were being torn apart.

Carol was a huge help and major support getting Ashley through the day. Mary came by early in the morning to take Steven home with her; Steven was allowed to skip school this day. By day's end, funeral arrangements had been made. Henry's funeral would take place Sunday morning at 7am. He would be buried in a plot beside his beloved Victoria, overlooking the sea they both loved.

After this, Ashley planned on attending church service at 10am, and then hosting the wake at Henry's house beginning at noon. On Monday morning, she had an appointment with Bill Jenks, Henry's attorney, for the reading of Henry's Will.

Sunday morning came too soon. The sunrise was obscured behind a thick fog. It was a slow drive to the cemetery. It looked as if the entire town was there to say good bye to Henry. As soon as the service began, the fog slowly began lifting. When the final words were spoken and it was time to lower Henry's casket, the fog was gone and the sun shone brightly on the procession.

Everybody attending the funeral also attended the church service later that morning out of respect for Henry. It was a full house at Henry's wake at the old house on the hill. To ease the burden on Ashley, people brought food and made it a potluck. Committed to making the wake a celebration of Henry's life, people took turns telling a story about one funny memory they had with Henry, then recalling a time Henry helped them, followed by a few words describing the conversation Henry had with them telling about finding Ashley and her return home.

The day went by quickly. All the guests lent a hand at cleaning up so Ashley would not have to. Then they all returned home, all except Carol. Carol wasn't a guest; she was family and invited to spend the night. It was getting late and Carol, Terry, Steven, and Ashley were getting tired.

"I think it's time to go to bed and get some sleep," Terry said. "You need rest, Ashley. Tomorrow is the final appointment. You are expected at Mr. Jenks bright and early at 8am so he can read your dad's Will to you."

"I need a few minutes to myself," Ashley said. "I'll be up shortly."

With that, all except Ashley retired upstairs and went to sleep. Ashley sat alone on the couch staring at the family photos on top of the fireplace mantle, thinking about her mom and dad, and her childhood at the home. She thought about how her dad had secured her financial future by purchasing a building downtown and paying for everything needed to open an auto-parts store. She thought about Carol trying to give them a car. She thought about how deeply her dad loved her, and how he, at his age, willingly took in Steven and was raising him the best he could.

Ashley began quietly sobbing; she did not want anyone to hear her because she wanted to be left alone. "Mom, dad, I love you. I'm so sorry I caused you so much grief. I hope you forgive me," whispered Ashley to herself. "I really need for you to forgive me. I can't live knowing how much I hurt you both. You were such great parents, and I didn't appreciate that. Please forgive me."

Then Ashley heard the creaking of the porch swing slowly moving back and forth. She went outside and noticed there was no wind; not the slightest breeze to push the swing. Then, in her mind, she heard Henry and Victoria's voice say, "We love you, Ashley. Everything is going to be okay."

More tears flowed down Ashley's face. She went back into the house, grabbed a pillow and blanket from the closet, went back outside, and sat on the porch swing. Crying, she said, "I love you, mommy. I love you, daddy." Then she lied down on the swing, head on the pillow, and covered herself with the blanket. Ashley slept there that night, crying herself to sleep.

Terry woke up first the next morning. It was just before sunrise and still dark outside. As soon as he noticed Ashley was not in bed beside him, he jumped up and began searching the house for her. She was nowhere to be found. In his search, he learned Steven was missing from his bedroom too. Then he woke up Carol.

"Carol! Carol! Wake up! Ashley and Steven are missing!" he shouted.

Carol popped up and immediately got out of bed. She put on her robe and ran downstairs as fast as she could,

"They're gone, Carol! Ashley and Steven are gone! What do I do now?" said Terry.

"Terry, I'm sure they're around here somewhere. Maybe they took a drive to the cemetery, or maybe they're down at the seashore together," Carol said, trying to calm down Terry. "Look for a note. Maybe they left a note."

Terry searched everywhere for a note – on the refrigerator, the kitchen table, the bedroom – and found nothing. Carol feared that Ashley, overcome with grief, may have grabbed Steven and ran away, but she did not share her concern with Terry because it would only compound the matter.

"No note," Terry said. "They ran off. I just know it. Ashley took Steven and ran off!"

"Don't be silly," Carol said. "Check outside to see if both cars are there. If not, I'll call the police station and ask them to have a look around town for them."

Terry took a peak out the window and told Carol that both cars were parked in the driveway. "Then I'm sure they're down at the seashore together. Grab a flashlight and let's walk down and have a look," Carol said.

Terry, in a panic, did not bother to grab a flashlight. Instead, he ran out the front door. The he saw Ashley and Steven cuddled together on the porch swing. He turned and went back into the house, and softly said to Carol, "I found them."

He motioned for Carol to follow him outside, which she did. When Carol saw Ashley and Steven, she whispered, "Let them be. Let them sleep. It's still not daylight. They'll wake up soon enough."

Just before sunrise, the birds began singing their morning songs. The chirping woke up Ashley. She looked at Steven, woke him up, and said, "Listen, Steven. Listen to the birds singing."

Steven opened his eyes, sat up, and hugged his mom. The two sat quietly for several minutes enjoying the birdsong until Ashley said, "Let's put on our shoes and head down to the seashore. Just you and me."

Steven nodded, and he and his mom did just that. They said nothing to Carol and Terry who were sitting in the living room drinking coffee when they entered the house. Ashley did not stop and give Terry a kiss on the cheek on the way out, and say "We'll be back." They grabbed their shoes and were out the door as quickly as they came in. Carol and Terry watched through the window as Ashley and Steven, hand-in-hand, made their way to the trail and then disappeared as they walked to the seashore below

"Ashley looked very happy," Carol said. "Let's give them some time. When they make their way back up, I'll start preparing breakfast."

Mom and son collected seashells together that morning. After experiencing the porch swing moving by itself and remembering what her dad said, she knew her mom and dad were with her in spirit and would always be watching over her and Steven.

The sun had now risen over the hillside and the seashore was bathed in morning light. It was time to gather the seashells they collected and go back home to eat breakfast. Ashley had to be at Mr. Jenks' office at 8am and Steven had to get ready for school. Steven asked his mom if he could stay home again today and his mom told him he had to go to school. Steven was disappointed.

"Do you think grandpa would want you to miss school again?" Ashely asked.

"No," Steven replied. "He wouldn't like that. But grandpa isn't here. Grandpa is gone now."

"No Steven, your grandpa isn't gone; he may be gone in body, but he's here with us in spirit," said Ashley. "He'll always be with you in spirit, watching over you and everything you do. Understand?"

"I understand," Steven said.

"Good, Never forget that. Always do and behave as if grandpa were beside you in body," said Ashley. "Okay?"

"Okay, mom," Steven said.

"Promise?" Ashley asked.

"I promise you, Mom," Steven answered.

"Good. Let's go. I'm getting hungry. Let's have breakfast and get you ready for school."

Mom and son walked up the trail to the house with seashells in their hands. When they got to the porch, Ashely stopped, looked at the swing, and said, "Good morning Mom! Good morning, Dad!"

"Why are you talking to the swing, Mom?" Steven asked.

"I'm not talking to the swing, Steven. I'm talking to my mom and dad; your grandma and grandpa," said Ashley. "Every day, whenever you pass by the swing, you should do the same. You should say "Hello," to your grandpa. And you should sit on the swing and tell him about your day. Can you do that for me, Steven? Can you do that for Grandpa?"

Steven nodded, and then said, "Mom, I'll be in in a minute. I want to talk to Grandpa."

Ashley smiled, began crying, hugged Steven, and went into the house. She said her good mornings to Terry and Carol and asked them if bacon and eggs, just like her dad used to make, were okay with them.

Steven sat on the swing, talking to his Grandpa. "Well. Grandpa, I have to go back to school today. I don't want to, but I know you want me to, so I'll go. It sure is a nice morning, Grandpa. Mom and I went down to the seashore this morning and collected a few seashells, just like you and I used to do. I had fun, Grandpa. Well, Grandpa, I better get inside now and eat breakfast and get ready for school. I'll talk to you later, Grandpa. I love you."

Chapter 15

The Last Will and Testament of Henry W. Benson

Carol drove Steven to school. She would meet Ashley at Mr. Jenks office after her business there was complete. Terry and Mr. Higgins were at the shop interviewing the first salesman while Ashley was with Mr. Jenks.

Bill Jenks worked from a home office in house located just a few blocks off Main Street. His house had been in his family for nearly 75 years. His dad was a lawyer, as was his grandfather before him. His dad was Henry's dad's lawyer, and his grandfather was Henry's grandfather's lawyer. There was a long-established trust between the families.

Ashley rang the doorbell and heard the sound and melody of beautiful chimes unlike anything made by any doorbell these days. She wondered if the chimes dated back to when the house was constructed nearly a century earlier.

Mr. Jenks opened the door and greeted Ashley. "Good morning, Ashley," said Mr. Jenks. Please, come in."

"Hello, Mr. Jenks," said Ashley.

"How are you holding up, dear?" Mr. Jenks asked.

"As well as can be expected," Ashley replied.

"Your father's ceremony and wake were beautiful," said Mr. Jenks.

"Thank you, Mr. Jenks," Ashley said.

"So, if you wouldn't mind following me to my office. Can I get you anything? A cup of coffee, perhaps. Or a glass of tea or water?" Mr. Jenks asked.

"No sir. I'm fine. But thank you, Mr. Jenks," Ashley said. "I just want to get this over with."

"I completely understand," said Mr. Jenks, who walked Ashley upstairs to his office. "Please, have a seat, dear."

Mr. Jenks took a seat behind a very large oak desk that seemed to take up the entire room. In her mind, Ashley pictured her dad sitting in the same chair she was now sitting in across from Mr. Jenks, dictating his final wishes regarding his estate.

"How is Steven holding up, dear?" Mr. Jenks asked.

"Surprisingly well under the circumstances. He's at school today. He wanted to stay home again, but I told him that his grandpa would want him in school, so he went without fuss," Ashley explained. "Carol drove him. I'm sure you're aware that my dad and Carol were engaged."

"Yes, I'm aware," said Mr. Jenks. "And Carol. How is Carol handling her loss?"

"Not well. She's devastated, which I understand," Ashley said.

"And your husband, Terry. He will not be joining us?" asked Mr. Jenks.

Ashley explained why Terry was not present and confided in Mr. Jenks that it was fine by her; that she really wanted to be alone during Henry's Will's reading. Mr. Jenks began by once again offering his condolences and followed with a few kind words reminding Ashley that their families have a very long history.

Mr. Jenks opened a manila envelope that sat upon his desk. On it was written, "HENRY WILSON BENSON. Inside was Henry's Will. He cleared his throat, took a sip of water, and said, "I've been doing this for over 30 years now, and it never gets any easier. The consolation for me is knowing I am carrying out the instructions of someone who trusted me to do so."

Before reading the Will, Mr. Jenks informed Ashley that her father directed him to read a brief note.

It read:

Since I have now found my daughter and grandson, and they are now both together, I request that before the Will is read both of them drive to Pines Road. At the top of the road, where the road ends, they will find an old mine that my father owned. This is where my father made his fortune.

After looking over the mine, please look down on the sea below. All of the land running along the seashore that you can see belongs to you. It was owned by my father, who gave it to me. Now I give it to you. To the two people, I love more than life itself.

Signed,

Henry Benson

On their way out, Mr. Jenks left a note on his door for Carol, who was going to meet Ashley at his office. Mr. Jenks drove Ashley to Steven's school to pick him up and take him with her to the top of the hill to look at the mine and the land below, as her father instructed.

This was a surprise to Ashley; Henry never once mentioned anything about a mine or owning land. She did know that her grandfather had made money in the mining business, but never knew where or how much money he had made.

The scenery on the drive to the mine was breathtaking, as was the view looking down at the shoreline and ocean below. Mr. Jenks stayed in the car while Ashley and Steven followed Henry's wishes. An old shack stood in front of the mine's entrance, which was boarded shut. An old, weathered sign was nailed just above the shack's doorway. It read, "Benson Mining Co."

Ashley and Steven found grass on the hillside and sat on the ground looking at the scenery below for nearly an hour. They did not say much to one another; there wasn't a lot to say.

Ashley took Steven by the hand and told him it was time to leave. On the ride back into town, Ashley told Mr. Jenks that there was no need to stop by Steven's school because she was going to let him miss the rest of the day.

When they arrived back at Mr. Jenks' house, Carol was sitting on his porch swing. Ashley asked Carol to mind Steven while she went upstairs with Mr. Jenks, who was ready to read her father's Will. Ashley and Mr. Jenks went back to his office and took their seats. The time had come for Ashley to learn what her dad wanted done with his estate.

After pouring a glass of water for both himself and Ashley, Mr. Jenks took a drink and then got straight to the point.

He read:

Last Will And Testament of Henry W. Benson,

Deceased

Filed October 1, 1958.

Last Will And Testament of Henry W. Benson

I, Henry W. Benson, a resident and citizen of Monterey County, California, being of sound mind and disposing memory, do hereby make, publish, and declare this instrument to be my last Will and Testament, hereby revoking any and all Wills and codicils by me at any time heretofore made.

If my grandson, for whose benefit a trust has been created hereunder, should die before attaining the age of twenty-five

(25) years, then the Trust created for my grandson shall terminate on his death, and all remaining assets then contained in said Trust shall be distributed outright and free of further trust to my daughter.

If my estate is the beneficiary of any life insurance on my life at the time of my death, I direct that the proceeds therefrom will be used by my Executor in payment of the debts, expenses, and taxes listed in Item I of this Will, to the extent deemed advisable by the Executor. All such proceeds not so used are to be used by my Executor for the purpose of satisfying the devises and bequests contained in Item IV herein.

Mr. Jenks read through the items and then said, "This concludes the reading of your father's Will."

Ashley was crying. Mr. Jenks consoled her until she stopped. Then he gave her the big news.

"Ashley, your father's estate is worth $25-million dollars. This figure is the sum of all land owned by the estate, investments, and cash in 10 banks," said Mr. Jenks.

Ashley nodded. She was unable to say a word. Mr. Jenks silently sat behind his desk as he placed his signature on several documents. Then he pulled a large manila envelope out from a drawer. In it were all the documents Ashley needed to show ownership over everything her dad left her.

When Ashley stopped crying, Mr. Jenks handed her the envelope and said, "This contains documentation transferring everything into your name. Look through everything when you're up to it. I suggest placing everything inside a safe-deposit box at the bank here in town for safe keeping."

Mr. Jenks then handed a second large envelope. On it was written, "BENSON ESTATE – COPIES." "Ashley, this envelope contains a copy of every document in the first envelope. This way you are you able to review everything without risking losing or damaging the originals," said Mr. Jenks. "And one final note, Ashley. Your dad paid me up front to answer any questions. You can call me any time to ask whatever question you have and don't need to worry about paying me for my time."

Ashley took the envelopes, stood up, and extended her hand to Mr. Jenks. They shook hands, and the meeting ended. Mr. Jenks escorted Ashley downstairs and out the front door to the porch where Carol and Steven were waiting for her.

"Take care, Ashley," said Mr. Jenks. "Good to see you, Carol. You take care too."

Carol had taken a cab to Mr. Jenks' house. She told Ashley that she was happy to take a cab back to the Inn so she could be free to do as pleased. Ashley would have none of it and insisted Carol come home with them.

Carol had class. She did not ask Ashley about the Will. She knew Ashley would tell her if she wanted to. Once home, Carol made lunch for them. After eating, Ashley asked Carol to accompany Steven and her to the beach below. As they walked along the shoreline, Ashley told Carol everything.

"My dad loved you dearly, Carol," Ashley said. "I love you."

"And I love you too, Ashley," said Carol.

"Carol, I'm giving you $1 million," said Ashley.

"No. I refuse to take a single penny from you," said Carol. "That's your money."

"Carol, please. If my dad was alive, I'm sure he would have shared what he had with you. Let me do that for him," Ashley said.

"No! Not a single red cent, young lady," Carol said. "I will refuse it. Don't make this any harder than it needs to be."

After going back and forth a few more times, Ashley finally got the message that Carol was serious; she was not going to accept any of Henry's money.

"I have you and Steven in my life. Stay in my life, and that's enough for me," Carol said.

The three of them then walked back up the hill to the old house. Ashley asked Carol to sit on the porch swing with her and watch Steven play in the yard. About an hour later, Terry drove into the driveway. His day interviewing salesmen was finished. Ashley did not mention the Will to Terry, and Terry knew better than to ask. Carol was invited to stay for dinner. After helping clean up after dinner, Carol went home.

That night, after Steven was asleep, Ashley told Terry what happened. They were rich, and he did not need to run an auto-parts store; they could relax and raise Steven. Terry would have none of that. He insisted that he carry out Henry's wishes and Ashley agreed.

Mars and Son Auto Parts officially opened for business two-weeks later. Ashley took on the role of a full-time mom. She went to Steven's school and introduced herself to his teacher and began volunteering in the classroom. She had Steven's last name legally changed to Mars.

Terry and Ashley invited Carol to spend Christmas Eve and Christmas Day with them, which she did. On Christmas morning, everybody opened presents. After that, Ashley asked Carol to have a look inside the stocking with her name on it hanging from the fireplace mantle. Inside her stocking, Carol found the key to the cottage next door and the home's deed made out in her name.

The Christmas card read, "Merry Christmas, Grandma. Welcome Home!" Carol began crying. She knew that she could not refuse the gift. It was Ashley's way of letting Carol know that she was a full-fledged member of the Mars family. From that day forward, Steven began calling Carol, "Grandma."

Chapter 16

Surprise!

Shortly after the reading of Henry's Will, Ashley decided not to touch anything in the house belonging to her father until New Year's Eve. When New Year's Eve came, Terry and Ashley worked together to itemize Henry's property and decide what to do with each item.

Carol thought it would be better for Steven not to be home when they removed his grandfather's clothes and personal belongings so she took Steven downtown for ice cream and a walk down Main Street before the shops closed early for New Year's Eve.

While Ashley was busy removing her dad's belongings from the closet, Terry entered the room with empty boxes. Terry knew it would be rough on Ashley to be in this same room looking at all of her dad's things. He offered to do the task for her but Ashley declined.

Next was the dresser of drawers. Henry removed each drawer, one by one, and placed them on the bed. As Ashley picked up each item, she paused as if to say good bye. Sometimes she stopped, held the item closely against her body, and told Terry a story about it. His blue and white Hawaiian shirt brought back the memory of the day the big blue couch downstairs was delivered. Henry was wearing the shirt that day. A pair of blue jeans with a patch sewn over the left knee brought back a memory of her dad building a planting box for the garden. Her mom grew radishes in the box.

As Terry was putting the empty drawers back into the dresser, he dropped one. It landed on the floor, upside down. There was a large envelope taped to the underside. He called Ashley's attention to the find. She walked over, removed the tape, took the envelope and had a seat. She asked Terry to turn over all the drawers to see if there were any more. There were none. Inside the envelope was a piece of paper with letters and numbers.

"What's written on the paper?" Terry asked.

"It says, L30 R40 L88 R25," Ashley said. "What does that mean? Maybe it must be some kind of a secret code."

"Sounds to me like the combination to a safe," Terry said.

"There's no mention of a safe anywhere in the documents from Mr. Jenks," said Ashley.

Just then, the old clock on the room's east wall chimed. The sound brought back memories of her mother telling her father how she hated that sound and wished he'd get rid of the clock. Ashley placed the envelope inside of a drawer in a nightstand in the room down the hall that she and Terry slept and then returned to her dad's room.

Next, Terry pulled boxes out from under Henry's bed. Inside were old family photos going back to her grandparents' days back in the late 1800s. It was opening a time capsule. Ashley took a break and went through each photo, one by one. Terry sat beside her and listened to her stories as she thumbed through the pictures.

She came across a photo of her dad and grandfather standing in front of the mine at the top of the hill she now owned. They were wearing miner's hats; the kind with the headlamp on the forehead. There were photos of miners standing beside small cars on rail tracks. These boxes and all the photos would be saved. Ashley and Steven carried them to their bedroom. She planned on looking through them all with Steven by her side tomorrow on New Year's Day.

After going through everything in Henry's room, Ashley suggested it would be a good idea to turn over each piece of furniture in case her dad taped more surprise envelopes to the bottom of more than just one drawer. Each piece of furniture, including the bed and mattress, were flipped. No more surprises were found.

The next room to be gone through was the basement. Three of the walls had ceiling to floor shelving units Henry built himself. They were bolted into the walls – Cambria was known to have an earthquake now and then. After all, this was California. One by one, each box was removed from its shelf and gone through. Nothing exceptional was found.

It was now 4.30pm and Carol and Steven were expected home any moment. It was time to stop going through Henry's personal property and time to begin preparing a special dinner for New Year's Eve. Carol and Steven arrived home at 5pm. Carol and Ashley busied themselves in the kitchen talking about their day, and Steven and his dad did the same in the living room. After dinner, everybody chipped in cleaning up the mess in the kitchen and washing, drying, and putting away dinner dishes. Next, it was time to sit by the fire and find an old movie to watch on TV together and wait for midnight.

Terry sensed something was the matter with Ashley; that something weighed heavily on her mind. When he asked her about it, she brought up the contents of the envelope they found taped to the bottom of the drawer. Ashley forgot all about it up until that point.

"Carol, did my father ever mention anything about owning a safe?" Ashley asked.

"Not a word, my child. Not a word," Carol said.

"Maybe grandpa found a safe filled with pirate treasure and it's buried under the sand at the beach," Steven said. The adults had a good laugh over the idea. "Or maybe he found a safe filled with pirate treasure and buried it somewhere in the backyard."

This got Ashley to thinking. She turned to Terry and said, "Terry, grab the tools you need to remove the bolts holding the shelving in the basement to the wall. We never looked to see if anything was taped to the back of the shelves."

Terry went outside to the toolshed next to garage and brought back a toolbox and lubricating oil; he knew there was a good chance the bolts were locked frozen over time. Terry instructed

Steven to bring a small box to place the hardware he was removing into so they didn't lose anything.

Each shelving unit was removed from the wall but nothing was found on the backside of them. As they were about to go back upstairs, Carol noticed that the wall that was behind one of the shelves looked different; it looked as if the plaster was a different shade of white than the rest of the walls.

Terry tapped a hammer along the walls. They sounded solid, like cement beneath a thin layer of plaster. When he tapped on the wall Carol pointed out, it sounded different; It sounded like there was wood on the other side of the plaster.

"Do you hear that? Do you hear the difference in sound," Terry asked. "I think we should remove the plaster and see what's on the other side."

"I trust your judgement," Ashley said. "What do you need to do that?"

"I need to go back to the tool shed and grab a few things. I'll be right back," Terry said.

When he returned, he had a sledge hammer and a crow bar. Wearing a pair of safety goggles, he instructed Carol, Ashley, and Steven to turn their back so flying plaster chips could not hit them in the face. With their backs turned, Terry lifted the sledge hammer and struck the wall. The impact sounded like a dull thump. Another blow and a thin layer of plaster about one foot square fell from the wall, revealing wood behind it. A third strike cracked the wood. A fourth hit and the wood fell into a hollow space on the other side of the wall.

"Hand me the flashlight, Steven," said Terry, who then shined the light through the hole. "Oh my God!"

"What?! What is it?!" Ashley asked.

"Did you find the pirate treasure hidden by grandpa?" asked Steven.

"It's a room!" Terry said. "Stand back everybody."

Terry began pounding on the wall, breaking the plaster, exposing a portion of the wall about the size of a doorway made of wood. Then he smashed the wood. During this time, Carol went upstairs and grabbed a broom. Steven shined the flashlight on what was once the other side of the wood, and to everyone's disbelief, there was an office.

"Everybody, come away until I've swept up. No telling what's on the floor. We don't need Steven stepping on a nail and have that go through the bottom of the shoe and into his foot," said Carol.

Once the pathway was clear, all four entered the hidden room that measured no more than eight feet deep by five feet wide. Against the far wall was a very old wooden desk. Next to it was a safe measuring around two-square-feet. Black and white pictures of the mine hung on the wall.

"Oh my," Carol said. "Looks like you've stumbled upon something."

"It looks like an office," said Ashley, who walked to the desk. "Terry, I bet the combination we found is the key to opening this safe."

"I'll get it and be right back," said Terry.

Sitting on top of the desk covered in a fine, thin layer of dust was a newspaper dated October 15, 1925. Ashley shined the flashlight upon it and blew off the dust. The headline read, "LOCAL BANKER CHARGED WITH EMBEZZLEMEMT."

"I've got the combination, Ashely. Let's get that safe opened up and see what's inside," Terry said.

"Not yet. Let's read this article first. But let's do it in another room; it's hard to breathe in here with all the dust in the air," Ashley said. "Hand me the envelope with the combination, Terry, and grab the rest of the paperwork that's on the desk."

They took the items upstairs and placed everything on the dining room table. Other than the newspaper, the other items were old bills and receipts. Ashley began reading the newspaper article aloud.

"This is from October 1925, Terry. My dad would have been 25 years old, and his dad in his late 50s," Ashley said. "The story says, "Yesterday morning at 10am, local police arrested Vice President of National Bank of Cambria John Mosely.

Mosley is charged with embezzlement of over $200,000 dollars. None of the money has been recovered. After booking, Mosley, 45, made bail set by Judge Mike Thatcher at $10,000 and was released. Judge Thatcher set arraignment for November 3 at 8am.”

“What does embezzlement mean, dad?” Steven asked.

“Embezzlement is theft, Steven,” Terry said. “Embezzlement is taking something that does not belong to you. It’s a crime.”

“Like pirates,” Steven asked. “Is that why pirates bury their treasure and hide it because the treasure is embezzlement?’

“Exactly, Steven. That’s exactly why pirates hide their treasure by burying it, because it is embezzlement,” Terry said.

“Do you think there is embezzlement in the safe in the hidden room in the basement, dad,” Steven asked.

“I don’t know, Steven, but we’re going to find out,” said Terry.

“If there is embezzlement in the safe, does that mean grandpa was a pirate?” asked Steven.

This comment made everybody laugh. Carol suggested she stay upstairs with Steven while Terry and Ashley went back downstairs into the basement to try opening the safe. Terry and Ashley thought that that was a good idea. It was better to keep Steven in the dark. This way, he would not be able to inadvertently open his mouth in mixed company and divulge what was found in the safe.

Terry held the flashlight while Ashley input the combination: L30 R40 L88 R25. They heard a click after the dial was spun to 25. Ashley rotated the handle and opened the door of the large black safe. She reached inside and pulled out several large envelopes. Inside were stock certificates dated October 17, 1921, which read, "Columbia River Gold Mining Company." The certificates stated that Wayne Richard Benson, Ashley's grandfather, owned 5,000 shares in the mining company. The stock was issued in the State of Washington.

A ledger book was among the papers found in the safe. Terry opened the ledger book and found many entries dated beginning on April 3, 1918. The ledger told the story of Henry's dad investing an initial sum of $1000 into the mine's operation – a hefty amount of money back in 1918. As he read down, he noticed entries of hundreds of dollars at a time being invested every few months.

As he read aloud, a story unfolded of Henry's dad repeatedly investing but never seeing a return on his investment. One after another, the entries were the same: money going out but none coming in. When he got to the October 1914 entries, he could see where Wayne purchased the Columbia River Gold Mining Stock.

An entry dated October 1, 1921 – 16 days before purchasing stock in the Washington company – showed a sum listed as an income of $25,000. Apparently, that must have been when Wayne struck gold. An entry dated November 14, 1921, showed another $25,000 coming in. Then again on January 18,

1922, another $25,000. This pattern continued every few months until the total reached $150,000.

Terry removed another item from the safe. It was a diary. It told the story of Wayne opening the Cambria mine to find quicksilver – mercury. Mercury was being discovered all across the area and was used in gold mining, which made mercury a valuable mineral. While Henry did not find any mercury in his mine, he did find gold. He struck an isolated vein – no gold had ever been found around Cambria before or since. Wayne kept his mouth shut about his find.

Wayne wrote about going to National Bank of Cambria for a loan and was turned down. The next day's entry told of Vice President John Mosely inviting Wayne to dinner. At that dinner, John told Wayne that he wanted to buy into his mine as a partner, but it had to be a silent partner. Mosley did not want anyone knowing he had invested in Wayne's mine.

Wayne agreed and they shook hands. The next day, Mosley brought Wayne $25,000 cash. It was just what the mine needed to buy more equipment. Time passed and John Mosley invested a total of $150,000 at $25,000 increments. Wayne's mine began profiting at the same time John Mosley was arrested for embezzlement; he had set up fake accounts and used that money to give to Wayne.

After being charged and released on bail, the next day, Mosley made a trip to the mine to speak with Wayne, the diary explained. Mosley made sure to arrive near sundown after the workers had left for the day so there were no witnesses to his presence. The two men met and talked at the mine's entrance. Henry was there with his dad.

Mosley, according to the diary, told Wayne that he needed the money back. Wayne told him he had no money to give back. The two of them started fighting. John fell down and hit his head on one of the ore cars sitting on the tracks outside the mine. The fall killed him, and Wayne and Henry buried John under where the miner's shack now sets. The diary went on to say that day after Mosley was buried, lumber was delivered and the shack built to cover the grave site.

A few days later, the newspaper reported that former National Bank of Cambria Vice President John Mosely had skipped bail and hadn't been seen. A few more days passed and the mine hit pay dirt; Wayne struck gold. He could not cash in on it locally; he didn't want anyone knowing gold was found in the local hills. He instead drove to San Francisco on weekends to cash in gold at different banks.

The facts behind their family's wealth uncovered by Ashley and Terry were never shared with Steven. Terry and Ashley wrote about what they discovered and placed the papers in a safe deposit box at the local bank. Steven found out about his family's past when he learned about the safe deposit box from his parent's Will.

Chapter 17
Doing The Right Thing

"Mr. Mars. Mr. Mars, are you awake?" asked the nurse.

"Yes, yes Mary," said Steven.

It is now December 2023. Steven is 72 years old and in failing health. He is at the cemetery visiting his grandfather, grandmother, mom, and dad. His mom and dad died in a car wreck on Highway 101 on New Year's Day 1999. They were driving too fast for the conditions. It was foggy. Terry had been drinking. They were returning home from a party.

Steven's live-in nurse, Mary, is by his side. She has been with Steven since 2017, when he suffered a stroke.

"I was just sitting here thinking about my childhood and my life," Steven said.

"It's time to go, Mr. Mars," said Mary. "It's getting late and the temperature is beginning to drop; we can't have you catch a cold."

Mary stood up from the white bench beside the graves and began pushing the wheelchair Steven sat in. Steven hasn't been able to walk for a few years now. Steven has been having Mary bring him to the gravesite every Sunday, rain or shine.

Steven was the last of his family. He had no children and never got married. He was the most eligible bachelor in Cambria but was very much the playboy well into his 50s. Steven helped his dad run Mars and Son Auto Parts until Steven closed it down after his dad died. They didn't need the money; they operated the store to honor Henry. The new owners had the building rezoned for residential and had it turned into three studio flats.

Steven has made sure that his family's secret is made public after his death. He has no children to worry about so no progeny will carry the burden of ill-gotten gains and face the scorn of the community. In his Will, Steven tells all. He reveals the location of John Mosley's body. Steven has arranged for the National Bank of Cambria to receive his fortune with instructions to create a public park on the beach and where his grandfather's house sits. The house is to be torn down.

This has been the story of Steven Mars, and his experience living by the sea.

The End

By Larry Hobson